Margaret West

# Search for a Stranger

A Pan Original

First published 1987 by Pan Books Ltd,
Cavaye Place, London SW10 9PG

9 8 7 6 5 4 3 2 1

© Margaret West 1987

ISBN 0 330 29645 0

Printed in Great Britain by
Richard Clay Ltd, Bungay, Suffolk

# Chapter 1

I charged out of Laura Ashley's into Sloane Street, and stopped dead. Peter was standing there, his back towards me, and he was seething. I didn't need to look twice at those hunched shoulders, those hands thrust into the pockets of his jeans. He was seething all right! I dived back into the shop.

It would be quite easy to dodge out behind him and make for the bus stop, leaving him to boil over without scalding anyone, especially me. I certainly wasn't in the mood for one of his tantrums today. It was tempting, but I glanced at my watch and realized he'd been waiting ages.

'Hi, Peter!' I called brightly. 'Sorry I've been so long.'

'Is that the lot then?' He glared at my carrier bags. 'You mean there's a slight chance we can go now?'

'I wanted to come shopping on my own,' I reminded him. 'I could have got the bus, and had more time—'

'*More time?* You've been *hours*! I had to feed the meter, and it's probably run out again, and I'm supposed to be home by six. Come *on*!'

We set off at a jog, with me panting, 'I didn't mean to be so long, but I can't hurry when I'm buying clothes. I *told* you that before.'

He grabbed my arm and jerked me into a side street, muttering, 'Car's up here. Honestly, Sarah, our last afternoon together, and you had to spend it in a dress shop! You know I've got to go to this stupid family gathering tonight, too!'

We turned another corner, the carrier bags flapping against my legs as I ran. 'I'm only going away for a *week*,' I gasped. It was bad enough keeping up this pace, without having to argue as well, but Peter seemed to be managing easily.

'Exams over,' he muttered, as we pounded on, 'summer holidays started, and you're off to Yorkshire, with me stuck here on my own!'

'You've known for ages that Mum has to go to this conference in Malta,' I said. 'And that she won't let me stay alone in the flat. It's only for a week, Peter, then we'll have some time together before Mum and I go to Florida.'

'Could have done your shopping earlier,' he grumbled. 'Could have kept this afternoon free. I've been standing on that pavement, watching the traffic, like a spare—'

'So why didn't you come inside when I asked you, and help me choose?'

'Oh, great! Nothing I like better than choosing girls' dresses. Naturally!'

'Right!' I said suddenly, surprising even myself. 'I'm going home on the bus.'

I spun round and raced down the street, with him pounding after me. He caught me at the corner struggling with the carrier bags.

'Sarah!' he yelled. 'Don't be childish!'

'*Childish? Me?*' I gasped. 'You're hurting my wrist.'

He relaxed his grip. 'Sorry. But I'm late already, and—'

'Okay, but you'd better cool it, Peter. I've apologized. Right?'

He nodded, and we set off again at a brisk walk back to the car. I hoisted one of the carrier bags under my arm. I could have used some help with my parcels, but I obviously wasn't going to get any from Peter.

He steered into the main stream of traffic, sighing, 'I expect, with you wanting to be a vet, you're looking forward to going to this farm. All the animals.'

'How many times must I tell you? I gasped. 'I've got no choice.'

'The other night,' he muttered, 'you were talking about the farm, and your grandfather, breeding horses. Sounded as if you couldn't wait to get there.'

'That's called "making the best of things",' I said. 'You could try it sometime. I also told you that the farm's in the Yorkshire Dales, and there's nothing in the village — no disco, no cinema, and the nearest town's miles away, with hardly any buses. How could I be looking forward to it?'

I spoke defiantly, but inside I *was* excited about my holiday in the country. I wouldn't let on to Peter, though. He'd never understand.

Peter fell silent, wearing his brooding expression. Why did I put up with him? He's great company when things are going his way, but sometimes I really do get tired of his moods.

I ignored him and concentrated on my own problems. Like the two dresses and three blouses I'd bought, not forgetting the lovely red skirt I'd found in Harrods. Mum wouldn't mind the cost, but she'd turn up her nose at the style. I could almost hear her voice when she saw them. 'Oh, Sarah! Not more peasant costume!' She'd say something like that, in a weary sort of voice, as if I was past hoping for. I was framing suitable replies in my mind, like, 'Well, at sixteen, I'd look pretty silly in the sort of clothes you wear!' I would, too. Look silly, I mean. For her job, something called Public Relations at the Royal Lancaster Hotel, Mum has to look supersophisticated. No problem for her, as she's tall, slim and elegant.

We'd reached Kensington Gardens when Peter broke his silence to say, 'And we can't go to Wales, either. Some holiday this is going to be.'

He'd had this idea of our going touring together in Wales, but Mum had said two words: 'No. Sorry.'

I sighed. 'You want to make me feel guilty about that, too? I *knew* Mum wouldn't agree. Look, I've got the message that I've spoiled our last afternoon together, and that you'll be stuck here on your own for a week. What have I got to do? I mean, like shave my hair off or something?'

We turned off Kensington High Street. He parked the car and came with me into the foyer of our flats. 'Can't come up,' he sighed gloomily. 'I'm late already.'

As he kissed me, I was surprised to feel a bit sad at parting from him. Well – maybe the afternoon *should* have been set aside for fond farewells. Peter was so nice when he was gentle, like now, looking at me with sad eyes like a puppy, and he was quite good-looking, and tall. I just never managed to live up to what he wanted of me.

'I'll be back in a week,' I murmured into his ear. 'And I'll write. You'll write back, won't you?'

He nodded and pressed the bell for the lift, kissed me

again, and as the lift doors closed, he was gone and I was alone, bracing myself to meet Mum's reaction to the dresses. Anything mid-calf, or with a full skirt, and she'll say something sarcastic, like, 'Just off to dance round the maypole, darling?' She ought to know best, but I know what I like and what I feel comfortable in. And I won't have my hair cut, either, which is another battleground. Nothing's easy.

To my relief, as I let myself into the flat, I heard Aunt Jane's voice. She's Mum's younger sister, a nurse at St Barnabas' hospital in the Cromwell Road, and she often drops in on Saturdays. Today, I needed her.

'Come on, show us what you've bought,' she demanded, snatching at the carrier bags. I laid out the dresses and blouses on the sofa, avoiding looking directly at Mum, who'd just got home and was wearing a cream suit with a pencil-slim skirt and black silk blouse. Good old Aunt Jane, plump and jolly, was wearing something shapeless in pink. Mum's given up on her sister ever since she gave her a Jean Muir dress she'd got tired of, and Aunt Jane wore it with a red leather belt and a green cardigan!

Anyhow, there was my lovely Aunt Jane, fingering the lace on the high collar of the blue dress, saying, 'Oh, if only I were young and slim again! These romantic dresses must be designed with you in mind, Sarah!'

'What?' Mum laughed. 'They're surely for the English Rose type – which Sarah certainly isn't! Still, I suppose she can get away with those styles, which is more than you can say for some people who wear them.'

While the going was good, I gathered up the dresses

to take them to my bedroom, and as I closed the sitting-room door, I heard something drop on the floor. My watch strap had broken again. I bent to pick up my watch, and heard Aunt Jane say, 'Well, at least he did one good thing, passing on his looks. Let's hope that's *all* she's inherited from him!'

'Oh, Jane, be fair!' Mum exclaimed. 'She could do worse than inherit his gentle nature, and he was gifted in many ways, too. Poor Jack!'

'*Poor Jack?*' Aunt Jane echoed. 'After all that trouble, you can say *that*?'

I hadn't meant to eavesdrop, but they were talking about my father, who'd died in a shooting accident when I was three. I couldn't remember him at all, and Mum would never talk about him. I stayed there, crouched, my watch gripped in my hand.

'It wasn't his fault,' Mum replied. 'If I'd been more sensible, more—'

'That's just it,' Aunt Jane said. 'He was older than you. Old enough to know he shouldn't marry you, for one thing.'

'Hey!' Mum laughed lightly. 'It takes two, you know. I took one look at him, and he didn't stand a chance.'

'M'm,' Aunt Jane murmured. 'I do know what you mean. Those smudgy dark eyes. That slow smile . . . But, Sally, I really do think that Sarah should be told, and I mean *now, before* she goes up to Yorkshire.'

'No,' Mum replied. 'Not yet. She couldn't handle it. When she's older, and been out in the world, then I suppose she'll have to be told.'

'And what if she finds out from someone outside the family?' Aunt Jane demanded. 'Imagine the shock.'

'Who's going to mention it?' asked Mum. 'Certainly not Mum and Dad.'

'Someone in the village, perhaps. Someone might say something, assuming she knew.'

'What?' Mum exclaimed. 'It's hardly the sort of thing you drop into a casual conversation, Jane! Besides, they'll all have forgotten. It was thirteen years ago! Let's do something about supper. I'm starving.'

Her voice trailed off as she went to the kitchen. I stood up, confused, anxious, as I always was on the very rare occasions that anyone spoke about my father. It was what was left unsaid . . .

I had a quick wash in the bathroom and looked critically into the mirror as I combed my hair. Aunt Jane said I looked like my father, but I'd no idea what he looked like. There were no photos, and that was another strange thing, really.

What was meant by 'smudgy' dark eyes? I thought of David Essex in those old films. I don't look a bit like David Essex. My eyes are very dark, and my long hair almost black. The art master at school had been droning on once about reflected light. 'Take Sarah's hair,' he'd said, and I'd nearly fallen off my seat because I hadn't been listening properly. He'd shone the spotlight on my hair, and everyone had gathered round to see how it shone blue. And I was the only one who couldn't see this phenomenon! Had my father's hair reflected blue light like mine?

'Not the sort of thing you drop into a casual conversation . . . She couldn't handle it . . . When she's older, then, I suppose she'll have to be told.' I shivered. It was creepy, just remembering those words.

Anyway, how did Mum know what I could handle?

# Chapter 2

Next morning, in bright sunshine, we were zipping up the M1 with Mum in her element, driving in the fast lane. It's boring being a passenger, especially on a motorway — even with Mum driving, which can be a hairy experience. My mind kept blotting out the car radio and recalling her words of the day before. Never had I felt such an urgent need to know about my father. Finally, I decided I had to know the truth before Mum flew off to Malta. Another whole week of worrying like this . . . No. I had to know now. Today.

When Mum's made up her mind about something, trying to change it is about as hopeful as asking the tide not to come in just yet. It was better if I could trick her into telling me more about my father, by asking a seemingly casual question that might just lead somewhere.

I raked my memory of the thumbnail sketch I'd been given of him over the years, searching for something to pinpoint — something I could hang a question on.

He'd come to Greenacres, my grandparents' farm, where Mum and Aunt Jane were brought up. He'd been sent by his employer to help with the harvest, in return for Grandad having lent his cowman to help with work on the other farm. He and Mum had fallen in love, and got married when Mum was only sixteen!

I dived in headfirst with, 'It's funny — I can't imagine

being married, at my age. I didn't even know it was legal. Didn't Gran and Grandad think you were too young to get married?'

She smiled. 'They did, and they were right. They did all they could to stop us, even forbade us to meet.'

'So you went on meeting secretly?'

She nodded. 'And they found out. I was too young to get married without parental consent, so I ran away to live with him in his cottage. The whole village was utterly scandalized. The permissive sixties had missed Thorndale out.'

She slowed the car a little to check signposts, then added, 'Since Gran and Grandad could hardly drag me back to Greenacres and keep me locked up, they gave in eventually, and we got married.'

'Romantic,' I murmured dreamily, praying that she'd go on talking.

'Ridiculous, more like,' she replied. 'I was silly and spoiled and had to have my own way. By the time you were born, just before my eighteenth birthday, I knew what a dreadful mistake I'd made. I hated having so little money, no new clothes, never going out at all.'

'Gran and Grandad were pretty well off,' I said. 'Didn't they help you?'

'I wouldn't accept anything,' she smiled. 'I had to keep on pretending they'd been wrong, you see, trying to prove it to them. Jack did his best. He made you a cot and a highchair and a cradle, all carved with leaves and flowers. He was so clever with his hands. But you know me – I'm hopeless at country life, even though at that time I'd known nothing else.'

I said, 'Perhaps eventually, my father would have got a job in a town, and—'

'Oh no!' she said. 'He was a countryman through and through. He'd never have survived in a town.'

This reminded me of something she'd once said when we were out in the country in early spring. I'd asked about some trees covered in pink blossom. 'Those are May trees,' she'd answered, gazing at the trees with a faraway look in her eyes. 'The day you were born, your father planted a May tree by the cottage gate, to ward off evil spirits. I often wonder if it's still there.'

But then she'd turned away and carried on walking.

'The shooting accident,' I murmured. 'How did it happen?'

Mum hesitated as she glanced in the rear-view mirror and changed lane. I sensed that my question had made her uncomfortable.

'He used to go out shooting rabbits,' she said finally. 'We needed them, for food. The gun went off accidentally.'

I got a mental picture of my sophisticated mum skinning and cooking a rabbit. It was pretty mind-blowing. I was trying to absorb the idea, when something flashed into my mind like a streak of lightning. The effect was about the same, too. SHE KILLED HIM!

I sat up, rigid, staring straight ahead. She wanted to be free. No one could prove it, because it looked like an accident. Oh, that was *crazy*! No! Mum couldn't have done it!

'What on earth are you looking at?' she asked suddenly.

I slumped back in my seat, weak with shock. 'Nothing,' I murmured. 'Except – the accident . . . I mean, could someone have shot him and made it look like an accident?'

Something told me this wasn't the right kind of conversation to be having on a motorway with the driver of a car going at this speed, but I was past caring.

'Sarah! Of *course* not! Jack had no enemies. What a ghastly thought! Several people saw it happen. Witnesses. Whatever made you think of anything so – well – *outrageous*?'

I took a deep breath. 'Last night,' I said, 'I heard you and Aunt Jane talking. And you've got to tell me what it is that's being kept from me.'

She glanced at me briefly. 'You listened at the door?' she asked sternly.

I explained about my watch strap breaking. 'Mum, please,' I begged. 'You've got to tell me.'

'You must have misunderstood,' she said. 'What did you hear us say?'

I repeated the entire conversation.

'Goodness,' she laughed. 'That *does* sound ominous!'

'Mum,' I growled, 'I know when I'm being treated like a three-year-old. Like now.'

'When you behave like one . . .' she replied. 'I really can't remember what we were talking about. I'm sure it would be something trivial. Your imagination just got out of hand.'

'It's not surprising, is it?' I snapped. 'Mum, I need to know what's being kept from me. I'm going to go on asking until you tell me.'

She pulled out and passed a Mercedes. 'Then this is going to be a very tedious journey,' she said. 'Perhaps

Jane thinks people in the village will remember my running away from home to live with Jack.'

'And I'm considered too young to handle *that*?' I asked.

'It's all I can think of at the moment,' she sighed. 'You know how Jane dramatizes things. You're getting to be like her in that way. It's time we stopped for lunch. I'll pull in at the next service station.'

I could feel the wall descend between us, like a sheet of plate glass, so that we could still see each other but communication was impossible. It often happened.

We were going to be on this motorway for a long time, and I wondered what it would be like if I kept on asking – on and on. She'd stop hearing me. I'd be like someone in a shop window, trying to talk to someone on the street.

The fact that she wasn't going to tell me, even now when I suspected there was something being concealed, was even more worrying. And I was stuck with it.

By three o'clock we were driving in steep narrow roads between dry-stone walls. 'Not bad going,' smiled Mum. 'We'll be there within an hour.'

I glanced at her profile as she slowed the car to drive through a pretty village of grey stone houses with lovely front gardens. She was as fair as I was dark. Hair styled at Vidal Sassoon, short and shining, the way she wanted me to have mine done. Just enough eyeshadow to emphasize the deep blue of her eyes.

'Have I got a smut on my nose?' she grinned.

'No,' I smiled. 'I was just thinking how different we are. I don't look a bit like you, do I?'

'No,' she laughed. 'You've got all the luck!'

16

I giggled. 'I mean, you look a bit like Gran. Aunt Jane looks a lot like Grandad. You're all fair with blue eyes, except me.'

'You're like your father,' she said, changing gear for the hill. 'And don't knock it. As far as looks go, he had the lot. Oh! Just look at that view!'

She meant, 'Over and out. No more questions about Jack.' Okay, I thought. I give in. No choice. I looked at the view, and it was breathtaking. We'd come over the crest of the hill and below us, the lush farming landscape spread to the Pennine foothills where the grass was emerald green on the slopes, and the sheep looked like tufts of cotton wool. Low dry-stone walls crisscrossed between fields, and pockets of woodland were cradled in the river valley.

Isolated farmhouses looked like tiny models made to fit inside matchboxes, and the sun glinted silver on a waterfall tumbling down a hillside.

A memory stirred deep inside me, and with it came a feeling of freedom that I experienced as a child when I stayed on the farm during summer holidays with Gran and Grandad.

'It's beautiful,' I murmured. 'But – I thought you didn't like the countryside.'

'I like looking at it,' Mum smiled. 'Living here is another story. Country life is damned hard, and very boring, as you'll discover for yourself, if you do decide to become a vet.'

She didn't want me to be a vet. Ever since I was in the school play, she'd had ideas about my becoming an actress. *Me*! The only character I can act is myself, trying not to bore people.

Mum drove over the little bridge that spanned the

river, and there was the big white farmhouse behind old oak trees, with mares and foals grazing calmly in the neatly fenced paddocks. Soon the car tyres crunched the gravel of the drive, and there were Gran and Grandad, coming down the three steps from the front porch to meet us.

The house always seemed enormous to me when I first arrived. As we went into the familiar sitting room I remembered how Greg and I used to play hide-and-seek, and it would take ages to find each other. Greg! I hadn't thought of him for years! He was the son of the local doctor, two years older than I. Last time I came here, four years ago, he was away on a school trip, so I never saw him at all.

Gran poured tea and offered home-made scones and malt loaf, and soon she and Grandad and Mum were talking about people I'd never heard of who'd died, got married, had children, or emigrated. I wondered vaguely what Greg looked like now. He'd be nearly eighteen! When we last played together, all through the long summer holidays, I'd be about ten and he'd be nearly twelve. I remembered him in shorts and Clark's sandals; curly yellow hair and freckles.

'Oh, Sarah! We're neglecting you,' Gran said suddenly. 'Another cup of tea? It's just that your mum has to go back tomorrow, but we've got you for a whole week, so we'll have lots of time to talk.'

I nodded, passing my cup. 'I was just thinking about Greg. Greg Anderson. Does he still live here?'

'Of *course*!' Gran paused with the teapot in midair, as if it was a really strange question. Then I remembered that people didn't move around so much here as they seem to in London. 'Greg's waiting for his exam results,' Gran said. 'Hoping to go to university, or medical school, I think.'

'Teaching hospital,' Grandad said. 'Going to be a doctor, like his father. Very tall boy, now. Good rugger player.'

That night, I lay in bed with the scent of rambler roses drifting in through the open window. Gazing up at the thick black beams that spanned the ceiling, I thought, *When Mum's gone back tomorrow, I'll ask Gran to tell me about my father.* There was no thick sheet of plate glass between Gran and me.

Mum had said to Aunt Jane, 'Dad and Mum certainly won't tell her,' but Gran and I had always been close. If she knew how worried I was . . . Suppose it was something awful, though? Aunt Jane had said it would be a terrible shock to me.

Suppose my father was a criminal? A murderer! Suppose – and a new thought sent a stab of fear through my body – suppose he was *insane*? Perhaps one day, I might inherit insanity! That was something Mum would avoid having to tell me for as long as possible!

The shooting accident – did he kill himself in a fit of madness? Or – and the shivers began to race through me – was he *still alive*, locked up somewhere, dangerously mad?

Mum hadn't married again; she met lots of men, and went out with them quite often, but there had never been anyone sort of permanent. She was so attractive, too. But what if she had a mad husband, guarded night and day, and wasn't free to marry?

It seemed an obvious answer as I lay there, trembling, trying desperately to think of plausible alternatives. Hereditary illness? He could have killed himself to avoid the suffering which he knew lay ahead – a dreaded disease had begun to take hold of him; a disease I would inherit one day!

No wonder Mum couldn't tell me, as we were hurtling along the motorway! But one day she'd have to, to prepare me. Perhaps when I was about to get married she'd tell me that I must never have children – or maybe I could never get married!

I was cold, though the night was hot and sultry. I drew the duvet close around me, shivering. Could I go to Mum's room, now, wake her up and tell her I just had to know the truth? But how could I face it? Wasn't it better not to know?

Outside, one of the dogs began to bark. The sound jerked me back to reality. I didn't *know*, did I? I was guessing. None of this might be true. 'Please, God,' I whispered, 'don't let it be true.'

The dog was quiet now, the air full of the scent of roses, and I began to breathe evenly again. The thudding of my heart was still pounding in my ears.

Then I recalled Aunt Jane's warning to Mum that someone might mention something to me, *assuming I knew*.

Relief washed over me like warm rain. You don't say to someone, 'I remember the day your father went mad', or, 'Oh, Sarah, I understand your father was a murderer.' And no one would 'mention' a dreadful disease that I was expected to inherit, would they? Not even 'assuming I knew'.

Yet Mum had said, 'It's hardly the sort of thing you drop into a casual conversation, Jane.' And that remark fitted in with my worst fears, didn't it?

Nothing seemed to hang together, and I was desperately tired. I was certain of one thing. Whatever it was, I had to know the truth. Someone was going to have to tell me, or I'd find out for myself somehow, even if I had to ask everyone in Thorndale. I'd find out, *somehow*.

## Chapter 3

I awoke the next morning to the sound of horses' hooves thundering over turf, and leapt out of bed to look through the window. In the adjoining paddock, the stable girls were exercising two huge horses. I recognized the big chestnut stallion. His name was Victor, and Claire was riding him. The other girl was riding a grey. Then I saw Grandad cantering along on a pretty black mare. He must be quite a few years over fifty, but he didn't look it as he let the mare break into a gallop.

Watching Grandad, I felt a sudden prickle of fear. The feeling took me by surprise until I remembered my horrors of the night before, and then a weight descended and lodged somewhere in my chest.

After a quick shower, I pulled on my jeans and thought, I'm an *idiot*! Lying in bed last night, tired and anxious, with the moon shining in through the window looking all spooky, I must have let my imagination off the lead.

My father locked in a padded cell? Insanity running through the family? There were other grisly possibilities, of course, but none so terrifying as the thought of the madman, in chains! I shivered. I still had to know the truth, and I'd watch out for any opportunity to ask questions, but I couldn't go on worrying about it all the time. The weight had gone from my chest now; the sun was brilliant. It was going to be a lovely day.

We waved Mum off at about ten o'clock. I told her not to drive too fast, and she laughed.

Gran and I went back into the big, stone-flagged kitchen and sat down to have more coffee. Gran passed the home-made biscuits and said, 'Well, Sarah, we must think of some outings for you, otherwise I'm afraid you'll be very bored here. Last time you came you were still a little girl, happy to be around the stables all day.'

'No, Gran, don't do anything special for me,' I said. 'Honestly — it's just nice to be here. And I'm longing to see the horses. Have you still got Brandy?'

'Oh, yes! Brandy's our best brood mare. She had two lovely foals this year. It was Claire who taught you to ride on her, wasn't it?'

I nodded. 'I saw Claire this morning, riding Victor. I'm glad she's still here.'

'Well, *of course* she's still here!' Gran exclaimed. 'You London people expect things to keep changing all the time! Claire's head stable girl now.'

'Oh, then she'll be too busy to let me ride Brandy.'

'Rubbish! Your grandad isn't a slave-driver. Claire can spare the odd hour or so. But do borrow a riding hat, and make sure it fits properly.'

I pulled on my wellies and went to find Claire. She

was sweeping out a stable, so I grabbed a broom to help. 'Hi!' I grinned. 'Remember me?'

'Sarah! I've been looking forward to you coming! Eh, but you're right grown up, now!'

I remembered then how I used to love to hear her talk, in her Yorkshire accent. She'd taught me lots of Yorkshire words, like 'beck' for stream, and 'mashing' tea, instead of making it. She used to laugh when I tried to copy the accent. I was hopeless at it.

As we swept the stone floor, she told me about the foals which had been born earlier in the year and asked me how I thought I'd done in my O levels.

Claire is a big, strong girl, but she looks very feminine and pretty, with blonde curly hair, grey eyes, and a fresh pink-and-white skin.

'I'll get Brandy saddled up for you after dinner, shall I?' she asked. She meant lunch, which was called dinner here. We turned on the hosepipe to wash down the stable floor.

'It wouldn't be fair, though, for me to take up your time,' I said.

'Give over!' she grinned. 'You'll help me out if I get behind with the work, won't you? You never did mind pitching in. I'll say this — I never expected a London girl to get stuck in like you did.'

'But I'm not a London girl,' I replied. 'I was born here. I'm as Yorkshire as you are.'

'Oh, aye!' she nodded, turning off the hose. 'I must be going daft! You was born in Hawthorn Cottage on Richardson's farm. But you've been brought up a city girl, not used to mucking out stables.'

I stood quite still, staring at her, doing mental arithmetic. Claire must be about twenty-five, so she'd have been around twelve when my father died.

'Claire,' I asked, as we wound up the hosepipe, 'what did my father look like? There aren't any photos, and I've often wondered . . .'

She glanced at me sharply, as if she'd just realized something. 'Well — I can't rightly remember,' she muttered. 'I was nobbut a schoolgirl, then. He was dark. Yes, he had very dark hair, like you. Well, that's the floor done.' She hung the hosepipe on its hook on the wall. 'Come and see Brandy. I wonder if she'll remember you?'

So Claire wasn't going to talk about my father. It was obvious from the way she turned to walk purposefully towards the end of the stable block. A cold quiver of fear shot through me.

My hands were trembling. I shoved them into the pockets of my jeans and said, 'What's Greg Anderson like now?'

She smiled, clearly relieved at the change of subject. 'Greg's a right bonny lad,' she said. 'You might see him later today. He usually comes for eggs on Mondays. He's just got an old car — a real old banger — but he's taken it to pieces and put it back together, and it goes a treat.'

I renewed my friendship with Brandy, then spent the rest of the morning helping Claire, which was fun because she has a great sense of humour. At lunchtime, she said, 'By the 'eck! We've shifted some work between us, and no mistake. I reckon I can take a couple of hours off this afternoon and come riding with you.'

After lunch we rode through the woods, out towards the moorland. Claire rode Brandy's stable companion, a quiet, much bigger piebald mare. We dismounted to sit by the river for a while and watched a kingfisher darting over the water, a brilliant flash of blue-green. The only sounds were the droning of insects and the ripple of water.

Claire told me that she was going to be married in the autumn, to Philip Thompson, the local saddler. She asked me if I had a boyfriend, and I told her about Peter.

'Why do you put up with him?' she asked. 'He sounds moody and downright disagreeable.'

'But when he's not in a mood,' I said, 'he can be super. Most of the girls at school have boyfriends. I'm not really bothered about having one, but it's useful, for discos.'

Claire looked astounded. '*Useful?*' she echoed.

'It sounds awful, doesn't it?' I admitted.

Claire gave me a disapproving look. 'Sarah! I'm surprised at you!'

I giggled. 'But Peter wants me for his girlfriend, so where's the harm?'

'You don't need me to tell you where the harm is,' she muttered darkly. 'You've no business just making use of people. Still, I don't see how you could be fond of a boy like that. It's time he started to grow up.'

It was good, talking to Claire. Not as if it had been four years since I'd last seen her. No need to be tactful or evasive. I could tell her anything, like how I'd decided I wanted to be a vet, and how Mum wasn't at all keen on the idea.

'Things you really want never come that easy,' she said. 'If you're sure that's what you want to do, then you'll just have to put your mind to it and accept that you'll have to manage without encouragement.'

She told me about a holiday she and Philip had had, in London, last year. 'It was a nice change,' she said, 'but we didn't like the smell.'

I stared at her. '*What* smell?'

'Fumes,' she answered. 'The traffic – it stinks. Petrol fumes and exhaust gases.'

'I've never noticed,' I said. 'I must have got used to it.'

'And the noise,' she went on. 'There's never a quiet place where you can't hear the traffic. But we loved Kew Gardens, and Hyde Park, and the National Gallery. Every evening we went out: to the ballet, the theatre – everywhere! So many things to do! Your gran is worried that you'll be bored stiff here, Sarah.'

I sighed. 'I know she is. But I won't. How can anyone be bored on a farm?'

It wasn't what I'd told Peter. He'd never be able to understand my love for the country. I hadn't realized myself how much I loved it until I'd got here.

'When you were little,' smiled Claire, 'you used to cry when you had to go home after the holidays. Even last time, when you were twelve, you cried at leaving Brandy.'

'I expect I will again,' I murmured, getting up to stroke the sturdy little mare. 'We've always lived in flats, where pets aren't allowed, or else it isn't fair to have them because there's no garden. I've always wanted a kitten. Actually, I've always wanted a dog, too, and rabbits and hamsters, and I've dreamed of having a horse.'

Claire laughed. 'If you get all those, you'll have no time to doctor any other animals!'

As we rode back into the stable yard, Claire pointed to a battered old Mini parked near the house. 'That's Greg's, car,' she said. 'You go on and find him. I'll unsaddle the mares.'

I raced into the farmyard. A hen was sitting on the bonnet of the car, and Greg was nowhere in sight. I almost giggled to myself, thinking of that scruffy little boy driving a car!

Then I heard a deep voice behind me. I spun round to see a figure coming out of the shed where the eggs were kept. The strong sunlight had cast deep shadows across the yard, so that I could make out only the shape of a tall man in faded jeans and a yellow cotton shirt. This couldn't be Greg. He was so tall.

He stepped out of the shade into brilliant light, and suddenly I was blinking stupidly at deep-blue eyes in a tanned face, short-cropped fair hair that crinkled where it was long enough to do so, and a wide, firm mouth, parted now in a smile that revealed white, even teeth. He was *gorgeous*!

'Greg?' I murmured faintly, still not believing it.

'Sarah! I'd have known you anywhere, even without pigtails!'

I felt my cheeks grow warm as I went on gazing at him — and I absolutely *never* blush! 'I — I wouldn't have known you,' I stammered. 'You — you haven't got freckles any more!'

He laughed and the sound was deep and husky, sending warm shivers along my spine. What was the matter with me? This was *Greg*. It was just Greg, who used to slide down haystacks with me. So why did his smile make me prickle, like a mild electric shock? And why was I standing here, tongue-tied, like an idiot?

He opened the car door and put the eggs into the glove-box. I had to make some effort at conversation. Mum was always telling me, when she had guests for dinner, or one of her drinks-and-bits-of-things-to-eat parties, that I must show an interest in people — ask them about themselves and make comments on what they told me.

I took a breath. 'This must be the car Claire was telling me about,' I said. 'She said you'd done a lot of work on it. You must be very good at mechanics.'

He grimaced. 'Not as good as I ought to be, to run a car of this age! Still, it goes quite well, now.'

'That's all that matters,' I said.

Gran came to the kitchen door and called, 'Come in and have a cup of tea with us, Greg. It's ready.'

As we crossed the yard, he said, 'I hope you won't find it too dull here, after London.'

Why did everyone think I was incapable of survival outside London? 'No danger of that,' I smiled. 'I've been out riding all afternoon, with Claire. Do you ride?'

'When I can afford it,' he replied. 'That means, not often. It's an expensive hobby.'

'It is,' I agreed. 'I'm lucky to be able to ride the horses on the farm. Perhaps you can come with me sometime.'

This was the way Mum had taught me to hold conversations, and it always worked. I'd never been more glad of her tuition than I was then, walking beside this good-looking stranger who used to be just Greg.

In the kitchen, Gran said, 'Well, you two won't be rushing around with bows and arrows this summer. Oh, bother! There's the phone. Sarah, give Greg some tea while I answer it.'

She dashed into the hall, and I poured the tea. 'Are you doing anything interesting during the holidays?' I asked.

'Not really,' he said. 'I've got a part-time job at a camp site just beyond the village. I help out generally, and work in the shop most mornings. When you go to boarding school you lose touch with local friends, so you don't get dragged into local activities – not that there are that many.'

'Maybe we should ask Grandad to make us some bows and arrows,' I smiled, offering him a scone.

He paused, about to take a bite. 'Oh! They were *ace*!' he grinned. 'I always thought it was incredible how he made the bows out of willow branches. Happy days! I often think of them. Do you remember the old sheep dog, Rex, who went everywhere with us?'

'Rex!' I nodded. 'He joined in everything. He even liked sliding down the haystack with us!'

Memories came rushing back. Greg reminded me of half-forgotten things and we chatted on and on, sometimes falling about with laughter. We must have sat there for an hour, reminiscing. I don't know what happened to Gran. Perhaps she deliberately left us alone together as part of her campaign to stop me from being bored.

Greg glanced at his watch and gasped. 'No! It *can't* be six o'clock! I promised Dad I'd mind the phone for him from six-thirty onwards. He's on call, but there's a hospital committee meeting at our house. Look, Sarah, if you've nothing arranged for tomorrow, I've got the afternoon off and we could drive out somewhere, or go into town if you like.'

'I'd like that,' I said eagerly. 'I'll have to ask Gran, but I don't think she's fixed anything.'

'I'll come tomorrow at two o'clock, then,' he said. 'Give me a ring tonight if you can't make it.'

I waved him off and stood by the gate, thinking how crazy it was to feel like this – excited and warm and happy – just because I was going out with Greg tomorrow. But it wasn't the Greg I'd been expecting. I mean, I knew he wouldn't be in shorts and Clark's sandals and about four feet tall, but nothing had prepared me for what he'd turned into. It was uncanny, and wonderful, and amazing!

I went back into the house, thinking, 'Please, God, don't let it rain tomorrow.' Greg had said, 'Not much point if it rains. We could go into town in the evening though, couldn't we? Tell you what: if it's pouring with rain, I'll ring you and maybe we can go to a disco or something.

A disco in the evening would be fun, but I went to discos all the time in London, and I wanted to do something special with Greg. I wondered how he felt about me. He'd said, 'I'd have known you anywhere.' Not much hope, then. I wouldn't have known him in a million years, but he still saw a skinny kid with pigtails, filled out in the right places but basically someone to slide down haystacks with.

I sighed, and took my writing case into the dining room to sit at the long table and begin a letter to Peter. I wrote, 'Dear Peter,' then sat staring at the paper. Well, Peter really isn't into country activities, like cleaning out stables or even watching kingfishers. When we'd talked about touring Wales and I'd said that it might be fun to go camping, Peter had scoffed: 'What's the point of living like gypsies when we can stay in good hotels?'

One of the golden labradors kept nudging my arm, hinting that I might care to take him out for a run. I liked the idea, so I braced myself and wrote about the journey up here, and what good time we made. (Peter loves fast cars.) Then I described the house. (Well, he's going to study architecture, so he might be interested.) I wrote that I'd been out riding all afternoon, then got stuck, and wondered if the letter was long enough. The dog was sure I'd written enough, and I decided I agreed with him and wondered how to finish off. I ought to write something soppy. I'd never written to Peter before, so this was a problem I was meeting for the first time.

In the end, I wrote that I had to take the dogs out and finished, 'Yours in haste, love, Sarah.'

'Right,' I said to the dogs. 'Let's go and post this.' They went mad with excitement and knocked over a vase of sweet peas, which I had to clear up.

Walking back from the postbox, I let the dogs off their leads to run in the meadow and leaned against a tall oak tree, watching them chase after sticks. I knew how they felt, because I felt the same: free and happy and full of energy. I remembered how, when I was little, I couldn't wait to get out into the meadow and race around, just for the joy of running. Gran used to say anyone would think Mum kept me tied up and shut in a cupboard at home!

Now, for a time at any rate, I was free of watching the clock, getting to places on time and, lately, the constant revising; the worry of wondering if I'd done enough work. I felt the rough bark of the old tree, hard against my back, and breathed the scent of the long grass. The setting sun was spreading gold and red across the sky, and the trees on the horizon were black shapes against a streak of orange.

Then, suddenly, something seemed to hit me hard beneath the ribs and my stomach contracted into a tight knot. Free? Happy? *Me?* So what was this dark shadow, closing in around me? I'd been able to keep it out of my mind all day, but now it was back, settling into the familiar dull ache in my chest.

I remembered Claire's reluctance to talk about my father; her hasty sideways look, her quick change of topic. Claire was no actress. She was honest and open — useless at pretending. If I'd needed proof that some secret was being kept from me, she'd unwittingly supplied it.

The dogs were at my feet, panting, waiting for the sticks to be thrown again. I picked them up. 'Last time,' I warned the dogs. 'Then we must go indoors.'

## Chapter 4

Gran was delighted when I told her that Greg had asked me to go out with him for the afternoon. I tried not to smile as she said, 'Such a nice, dependable boy, dear. You'll be quite safe with Greg.'

To my relief the weather was warm and fine again, so Gran insisted on packing a picnic for us. 'Greg has no mother, and his father's housekeeper is kept very busy. I phoned her to say I'd do a picnic for you. It's so expensive to go to cafés.'

I nodded in agreement as I went upstairs to put on my blue Laura Ashley dress for the first time. Ripples of excitement kept racing through my body. 'Stop this!' I told myself sternly. 'It's only Greg. *Greg* — remember? You used to play kids' games with him.' Cowboys and Indians, in actual fact. Greg and I would dash about chasing outlaws and escaping from Indians, with Rex barking all the while.

Remembering all that made no difference. The boy I'd played with had nothing to do with the tall young man I was going to meet downstairs in just a few minutes.

We drove over the little bridge and through the village, on to the road that ran beside the river, talking easily all the way. We discovered that we liked the same kind of music, had read the same books. We disagreed about some things, and argued, and came halfway to seeing each other's point of view. It was all relaxed and interesting.

The scenery was spectacular. The sun blazed down. The river had dwindled to little more than a stream when we reached the higher ground and we stopped, leaving the car in a lay-by, and walked to the bank, where we sat for a while and went on talking. Then we gazed into the fast-running water, watching the little silver fish dart between the brown pebbles on its bed. It was still and quiet, as if we were the only two people alive.

We wandered further up the hill, to where the stream became a waterfall tumbling down the rocky face of a cleft. Greg said, 'My father once saw a salmon leap this waterfall.'

He was surprised that I knew about salmon fighting their way up river to lay their eggs in fresh water. 'You can recognize more birds than I can, too,' he said. 'It must be awful, living in a town and being so interested in nature.'

We crossed the stream lower down, stepping on smooth, rounded stones, barefoot because the water was racing fast, throwing up spray. Greg took my hand, leaping on ahead and guiding me to each stone. Not that I needed it, but it was nice. I'd noticed this attentiveness in the men with whom Mum sometimes went out. They'd take her coat, carry parcels, open doors. I'd often wished someone would give Peter a crash course in gallantry, or whatever it was called nowadays.

I don't know what happened to time that afternoon. It simply flashed past, like the silver fish in the stream. All we did was walk, and sit, and talk.

I told Greg about my hopes of getting into veterinary college, and asked where he would do his medical training.

'What I'm really praying for,' he grinned, 'is St Barnabas', but everyone wants to go there. I've nearly killed myself trying to get the exam results they want. Two As and a B is the least they'll take.'

'Barney's?' I gasped. 'But – that's not far from where I live! My Aunt Jane is a ward sister there! Oh, Greg, you must get into Barney's – you *must*!'

'I keep trying not to hope,' he sighed. 'It's like tempting fate.'

I nodded. 'Yes. We must be very careful. We'll keep saying it's hopeless and impossible, and throwing salt over our shoulders, and never walking under ladders. If I had a good-luck charm I'd give it to you, but I haven't.'

He laughed and put an arm across my shoulders, pulling me close to him. 'You are a nut!' he grinned. And then he kissed me.

It was so unexpected. It had always seemed a bit of a nuisance before when boys wanted to kiss me, Peter included. I'd put up with it out of politeness. But this was *so* different! I put my arms around his neck, wanting the kiss to go on and on.

When we drew apart, I still had this warm feeling running up my spine. 'Isn't it strange,' I murmured, 'how things change?'

'You mean, you and me?' he replied. 'Well, Sarah, we go back a long way.'

I giggled. 'That sounds like a line from an old American film, but I know what you mean.'

'I like old American films,' he said. 'You know where you are. Good guys and bad guys, and the good guy always wins. That's how things ought to be.'

That set us off on another long discussion, until I glanced at my watch. 'Oh no!' I muttered. 'My watch has gone wrong again. It says half-past five.'

Greg checked his watch. 'That's the right time,' he said. 'I don't see how it's possible, but we can't both be wrong. Shall we get the picnic?'

We brought the basket to the riverside and ate Gran's ham and tomato sandwiches, seed cake, fruit cake and pears, and went on talking. I'd never talked so much to anyone before.

'What would you like to do now?' asked Greg, as we finished putting things back into the basket. 'There's a good disco in town, and I think there's a folk club on Tuesdays. Or there's the cinema, but I don't know what's showing.'

'Do you want to go into town?' I asked.

He hesitated long enough for me to guess, then said, 'Yes, if you do. You decide.'

'I'm not dressed for a disco,' I said. 'And in this weather, it's so nice out here . . . But if you want to go into town—'

'I could just go on sitting here, getting to know you,' he smiled, and my heart began to race. I couldn't get used to the effect he had on me.

'We could drive around,' he suggested. 'There are some interesting old villages. There's one with the original village stocks in the High Street. They keep threatening to bring them into use again, for vandals!'

I laughed, then said, 'There is a place I'd like very much to see, back near Thorndale. A cottage. The house where I was born.'

'Right.' He picked up the basket. 'Let's go.'

As we walked back to the car, I said, 'But I don't know where it is, except that it's outside Thorndale, nearly into Allandale. It's on land belonging to Richardson's farm. Oh – and there's a May tree growing by the gate – if it's still there. It was planted sixteen years ago.'

'It takes a lot to kill a May tree,' Greg said, 'but I don't know Richardson's farm. Funny – I should know all the farmers around here.'

We stopped in Thorndale to ask directions to Richardson's farm. The butcher, just closing his shop, said, 'That'll be Lockwood's farm. Old Mr Richardson died, must be ten year back. Billy Lockwood took it over. Go on for about a mile, till you see the pillar box, then turn left, then take first left and first right.'

'It's actually a cottage we're looking for,' I told him. 'You might know it. Hawthorn Cottage.'

'Oh, yes. Reg and Mary Barton's place. You won't find them in. They're at the village hall – meeting of the Young Farmers' Club. Mary does the refreshments.' He picked up a long pole to push back the shop sunblind, and hooked it on to the catch.

'Thanks,' I said, 'but we just want to look at the cottage. I was born there.'

The blind swung back. He unhooked the pole, and looked at me with a puzzled expression. '*Born* there?' he repeated. Then he blinked and looked at me, as if he was seeing me for the first time. 'You mean – but then, you must be Jack's girl! Jack and Sally Leigh's daughter!'

I nodded hopefully. 'You knew my parents?'

He was still looking at me, with the same puzzled expression. 'It were twelve, no, thirteen years ago,' he murmured. 'Yes. I knew them. Yes. Go the way I've told you, but go past the farmhouse and take your first right turning off the lane. Best not drive down there, though. It's a rough old track. Ruin your springs.'

Greg thanked him, and the butcher turned and went quickly back into his shop and closed the door. As we drove off, I looked back and saw him watching us through the shop window, staring as if he couldn't believe his eyes. I shivered.

'What did he mean,' Greg muttered, 'it was twelve or thirteen years ago? The accident, I suppose. Your father was killed in a shooting accident, wasn't he?'

'Yes,' I murmured. 'How did you know?'

Greg wrinkled his brow. 'I can't remember. Some-one must have told me, because we only came here ten years ago. You know how it is in a village. Everyone knows everything.'

'Except me,' I heard myself say. My hands were still trembling. The butcher's attitude had been the same as Claire's.

'What do you mean?' Greg asked, surprised.

I hesitated. But this was Greg, and surely I could tell him?

'All I know about my father,' I said, 'is that my grandparents disapproved of him, and he died in a shooting accident. I overheard something accidentally, quite recently. My Aunt Jane was saying to my mother that I ought to be told something, but Mum won't tell me what it is. It's been worrying me ever since.'

Greg slowed the car and turned into a narrow lane. 'Usually,' he said, 'these things turn out to be quite trivial. You hear part of a conversation, and—'

'No, Greg, not this. My mother said I was too young to cope with whatever it is. And that butcher is the second person to close up tight when my father's name is mentioned. *This* is what I can't cope with – the mystery. I don't even know what my father looked like. There are no photos. I – I just need to know about him.'

'Of course you do,' replied Greg, quietly. 'He was your father.'

He said it as if it were a simple fact. I gazed at his profile as he steered the car carefully down the narrow lane with high hedges on either side. I felt tears stinging my eyes. I'd never dreamed that anyone would under-stand how I felt.

Greg said, 'I can't remember my mother at all, but there are photos, and my father talks about her often, and I've got things that belonged to her. It would be awful, knowing nothing about her.'

There was a tightness in my throat, but I was determined not to cry. 'He planted the May tree,' I said, 'on the day I was born – to ward off evil spirits. Is that an old country superstition around here?'

'It could be,' he answered. 'There are lots of legends about the May tree. It was believed to be the tree used to make the crown of thorns at the Crucifixion. To the Greeks, it was an emblem of hope. My father once told me that if there was a May tree with a hole in the trunk, people would bring a young child and pass it through the hole – it was supposed to cure things.'

'I didn't know that,' I said. 'I just knew they used the flowers for the May Queen's crown in villages where May Day is celebrated. Do you believe in things like that? Do you believe in evil spirits?'

'I've never thought about it,' he replied. 'But if there's anything that's supposed to ward them off, then I'm all for it.'

We both laughed. That was the thing about Greg – he never ridiculed anything. Peter always had strong opinions, about politics and all sorts of things, and thought he was right about everything, which made everyone who didn't agree with him not only wrong, but stupid as well.

We passed the farmhouse and went on until we came to the turning. 'The butcher was right,' Greg said. 'Better not drive down. I'll reverse and park here.'

He backed off into the entrance to a field, and we left the car and walked down a path that was little more than a cart track. Soon we saw the cottage, and I hurried forward to the low white picket fence that surrounded it.

The house was small and square, built of the local grey stone, with a blue slate roof and blue-painted window frames and door. There was a porch over the door tiled with blue slates, and the tiny front garden was bright with flowers. Beside the gate was a May tree, about fifteen feet tall and sturdy, with a gnarled trunk and wide-spreading branches dense with leaves.

I leaned over the fence to put my hand on the rough bark of the May tree's trunk. 'I wonder if the blossoms are pink or white?' I murmured.

'I'll come and look at it next spring,' smiled Greg. 'I'll let you know.'

We both turned at the sound of a tractor coming down the lane. As it drew near, the driver stopped and called, 'If you're looking for Reg and Mary, they're down the village.'

'No,' I answered. 'We were just – walking.'

He nodded. 'That your Mini back up there?'

'Yes,' Greg answered. 'It's not in the way, is it? I didn't want to risk my springs.'

'Very wise,' the man smiled. 'No. It's not in the way. Looking at the cottage? Pretty little place, isn't it?'

'Yes, it is,' Greg answered. 'My friend' – he put an arm across my shoulders – 'was born here. Her father planted that May tree.'

The man stared at me, then said slowly, 'It was Jack Leigh planted that May tree. Jack Leigh was your father?'

'Yes.' I felt my heart quicken as I returned his gaze.

He went on staring at me, a smile hovering at his lips.

'So you're that little baby! All grown up now. Oh yes! Yes, I can see Jack in you!'

'You knew him?' Greg asked.

The man nodded. 'Everyone around here knew Jack. I never knew anyone like him. Good with animals. A farmer would send for Jack before he sent for the vet. Jack would always know what to do, and he could cure an animal with herbs. He'd know if it was a job for the vet, though – never took no chances. And musical! He could play the violin fit to tear your heart out, though he'd never had a lesson. Still, you'll know all that, Miss, won't you?'

'No,' I murmured. 'No, I don't. I was only three years old when he died, so—'

Abruptly, the smile left the man's face. 'Aye – terrible thing to happen. Terrible!' He started the tractor and, above the noise, shouted, 'You'll be staying up at Greenacres, then, with your grandparents?'

'Yes,' I whispered, knowing that he wasn't going to talk to me any more.

'Well, have a nice holiday, then, Miss. I'd best be getting on. What was it they called you? Sarah, was it? Yes, Sarah.'

The tractor chugged on down the lane, and the man lifted his hand in a wave.

I gazed after him. 'It's always like that, Greg. They look sort of – scared. Did you notice?'

'Perhaps they're embarrassed,' Greg said. 'Because he's dead. I've noticed often that relatives sometimes refer to my mother, then look at me and gloss it over, as if they've said something wrong.'

'No, I'm sure there's something more.' I shivered. 'Maybe he was a criminal of some sort. Maybe he killed someone. Oh, Greg, I *must* find out. I must *know*. What can I do?'

We walked slowly back to the car and sat inside for a time, not speaking, then Greg said, 'If he died here, then he must be buried here. We could look for his grave in the churchyard.'

I turned to him, full of gratitude. 'Oh, Greg! Could we go now?'

He started the car. 'It won't tell us anything, though,' he warned. 'We've got to find a way of getting someone to talk about him.'

As we entered the village, I said, 'The vicar! He would be the right sort of person to ask!'

Greg shook his head. 'The present vicar is new to the parish. Reverend Haywood retired and went to live in Hastings.'

We parked the Mini and walked through the lych gate into the churchyard. Most of the graves were very old, with headstones leaning at strange angles. 'Perhaps it's not used now, for burials,' I said. 'Some of these graves are over a hundred years old.'

'There are more recent ones behind the church,' Greg said. 'But – well, he could have been cremated. Most people have cremation, now.'

We followed the narrow path to the back of the church and examined the gravestones, but there wasn't one for my father, and running through my mind was the thought – perhaps he didn't die. Perhaps he's still alive.

We sat on the low stone wall that surrounded the churchyard, shaded by tall yew trees.

'It was lovely to see the cottage,' I smiled. 'Thank you, Greg, for taking me.'

He put his arm around me. 'We haven't got any-where with your problem, though,' he sighed. 'We must both think hard about it. There's sure to be a way.'

'Like asking my grandparents outright,' I said. 'But if they refuse to tell me, or just fudge around it like everyone else, then it'll be worse than not having asked.'

'If they wanted to tell you, they'd tell you,' said Greg. 'We've got to find out on our own. How long have we got?'

'What? Oh – I'm here for a week,' I replied.

'A *week*?' He looked at me, startled. 'I – sort of – thought you were here for some time. You used to stay for the whole holidays.'

'I'm only here while Mum's in Malta, on a confer-ence,' I said. 'I'd like to stay longer. I could ask Gran if I could stay for an extra week, but after that I have to go on holiday with Mum and Aunt Jane. We're going to Florida. It's all fixed.'

Then, suddenly, I was telling him about the holiday Mum had arranged – telling him that I didn't want to go. Until then, I hadn't actually realized that I didn't.

'Because Mum works at the Royal Lancaster,' I said, 'there are, sort of, reciprocal arrangements – perks. We stay at really classy hotels, where they think of every-thing you might possibly want. Everything's done for you almost before you know you want it done.'

'And that's why you don't want to go?' he grinned. 'Of course, I appreciate what a dreadful hardship all that must be—'

We both laughed. 'I know – I'm crazy. I hate having to dress up all the time, and Mum and Aunt Jane worry

43

in case I'm bored, being stuck with them, but I'd *rather* stay with them. As soon as we arrive, they start looking out for someone of my age who might be suitable as a companion for me. If it's someone I don't like, it's awful.'

'I can imagine,' Greg nodded.

'Last year,' I went on, 'in Rio, there was this spotty American boy called Walter. Into geology. Kept on and on about strata, and rocks. I'd rather be free to look around, but everything's always so *organized*.'

'Even with Walter?' Greg grinned.

'*Especially* with Walter! He had maps and diagrams and wanted me to go to places where they've discovered interesting layers of rock! He went jogging every morning and evening, and swam a certain number of lengths in the pool every day. He was a very nice guy, really, but I got close to hating him.'

'What do your mother and aunt do on holiday?' he asked.

'Aunt Jane likes the beach. Mum finds out how the hotel is run. In the evenings they see a play or a show which they say I won't like, and they insist I go wherever the other young people in the hotel are going. We look at whatever tourists are supposed to see in the area. I like that. It's the only time I don't feel I'm being a drag.'

'You couldn't be a drag,' he smiled. 'But why not tell them you don't want to go to Florida?'

I gasped and turned to look at him. 'Oh, Greg! I *couldn't*!'

'Why not?'

'Well — it would be so ungrateful! It would be hurtful, wouldn't it? And it would be pointless. I've got to go. Mum wouldn't let me stay in the flat alone, so where would I go?'

'What about here, at Greenacres?'

I smiled. 'Oh, Greg, I'd love to stay here for all that time! A whole *month*! But maybe Gran wouldn't want me for that long. And I could never tell Mum I didn't want to go on holiday with her.'

'Surely,' Greg frowned, 'if she knew you'd rather stay here, she wouldn't mind? She's got your aunt to go with, so she wouldn't be on her own.'

I shook my head. 'I just couldn't tell her. It would be cruel.'

He shrugged. 'Well, I don't know your mother, so . . . But I know Dad wouldn't want to drag me along on one of his golfing holidays.'

'You go on school holidays,' I said. 'And you've got a housekeeper, so he doesn't have to worry about where you can stay while he's away. You can stay at home.'

'Yes,' he nodded. 'I can see it's quite a different situation.'

As he said that, I began to wonder. Was it all that different? If Gran would let me stay here . . . Aunt Jane would understand. Maybe I could phone her and ask her what she thought . . . Then I pushed the idea out of my mind. It was selfish. Mum wanted to give me a super holiday, and I ought to try to enjoy it.'

Strains of country music interrupted my thoughts. The sounds drifted across from the village hall behind the church. 'Looks like party time over there,' Greg said. 'I thought it was supposed to be a meeting of the Young Farmers' Club tonight.'

The doors of the low stone building stood open,

with light spilling out into the car park. 'Sounds good,' I smiled. 'Country and Western.'

'Let's go and look,' he shrugged.

'But it's private, isn't it? We couldn't go in, could we?'

'I know a few young farmers,' Greg grinned. 'They can only throw us out.'

They didn't. They dragged us in, forcibly. We hovered for a bit at the door until I got embarrassed and wanted to leave, but Greg took my arm and said, 'Hang on a minute. I'll attract someone's attention.'

A stocky young man of about twenty caught sight of us and came to the door. Greg said, 'Hi, Rod! So this is how you hold a serious meeting of the Young Farmer's Club!'

Rod laughed. 'This is our monthly barn dance. Come on in. And don't bother to introduce me to your gorgeous partner, will you?' He smiled directly at me, and his eyes were cornflower blue against his tan.

Greg introduced him as Rod Oakroyd, and I said, 'You all seem to be having a good time in here.'

'It's parole from hard labour,' he replied. 'Greg will tell you that farmers are just a lot of lazy layabouts, but it's not true.'

'Then I won't believe him,' I promised.

Several more people had drifted to the door to see what was happening. Rod turned and said, 'Gate-crashers here. Who's going to help me chuck Greg out?'

Amid good-natured cries of 'Push off, Greg!', 'You grab his arms, and I'll take his feet . . .', we were grabbed and pulled into the hall.

After the caller had announced the next dance he

looked straight across to where Greg and I were standing, near the doors, and said, 'Young lady in pretty blue dress, tall young gentleman in red shirt, come forward please, and take your places. Now, honour your partners . . .'

And we were off, skipping round the hall, changing partners, finding each other again; it was great! Everyone was so friendly, as if they'd known us for years — well, of course they *had* known Greg for years. I'd forgotten how, in the country, people are so nice to you, even if they don't know you.

In the Ladies' I was talking to Rod's girlfriend, Alison, saying I didn't know there were so many young people living in Thorndale. 'No,' she said, 'they come from far and wide, some from villages forty miles away.'

She told me she was training to be a shepherdess. I said, 'What — like those in the sheepdog trials on television? But they're all men!'

She laughed. 'Oh, Sarah! You must have seen those pretty porcelain figures in antique shops — "Shepherdess with lamb". Goodness knows how they managed in those lovely long dresses and white petticoats, though. My dad's been a champion shepherd for many years, and now he's training me. We breed our own sheepdogs. Come and see our new puppies sometime.'

'Thanks, I will,' I nodded. 'But, Alison, that television programme is called *One Man and his Dog*. If you get into the trials, they'll have to change the title.'

She laughed. 'One person, and his or her dog, or bitch.'

The caller had started again. We dashed back into the hall.

*

It was midnight when Greg drove me back to Green-acres. As the car stopped in the drive I stared in dismay at the farmhouse. Not a light to be seen!

'Ouch!' I gasped. 'They've all gone to bed! I forgot about farmers having to be up early. I'll have to knock on the door if it's locked, and wake them up! Oh, Greg, Gran will be cross about this!'

'No she won't,' he smiled. 'I meant to tell you: when you went off with Alison I phoned your Gran to ask if we could stay until the end. She said not to worry, and she'd leave you a note on the hall table about bolting the front door. She promised not to wait up.'

'Oh!' I breathed. 'Thank heaven! What made you think of doing that?'

He laughed softly. 'I *live* here, you nitwit! This may seem like halfway through the evening to you, but farmers have to be up at the crack of dawn.'

He came with me to the front door and said, 'I've got to work tomorrow, Sarah. I've a full day on Wednes-days, but I'll ring you when I have another free after-noon, if that's okay with you.'

'Yes, please,' I smiled up at him. 'Thank you, Greg, for a lovely time.'

He kissed me gently and said, 'I'll wait in the car until you're inside the house, with the door bolted.'

I stepped inside and flicked on the light, then turned to give Greg a quick wave. I read Gran's note and did as instructed, standing on the chair to push home the top bolt. I switched out the hall light and heard Greg's car start, and then the tyres crunching the gravel of the drive.

Soon I lay in bed, thinking about Greg. Was he really working tomorrow, or was it an excuse not to see me again? Suppose he didn't ring, and I never saw him again? Life couldn't be so cruel, could it? Surely I'd have known if he'd been bored with me?

I closed my eyes and imagined we were sitting by the stream, watching the tiny silver fishes making their swift darting movements between the pebbles. Later, when we sat on the low wall of the churchyard, he'd held my hand . . .

Something was tugging at my memory, trying to get in, and I wouldn't let it. All right, I had a big problem to sort out: something awful that I had to face eventually, but not now. It could wait. Nothing must spoil this lovely day.

I'd be like Scarlet O'Hara, in *Gone with the Wind* — I wouldn't worry about it tonight; I'd worry about it tomorrow.

# Chapter 5

Gran didn't mind at all that I'd stayed out late. 'So long as we know where you are, and whom you're with,' she said, 'we shan't worry.'

'I had a super time,' I said, weighing out the fruit for the cake Gran was making. 'Everyone was so friendly, especially Rod and Alison. Did you know that Alison was training to be a shepherdess?'

'Yes. I'm sure she'll do well. They breed border collies, you know.'

'Alison invited me to go and see the puppies,' I said.

'When can I go?'

Gran smiled. 'Whenever you like, Sarah. You're quite free to do as you please. I know your mother has to be very careful, in London, where you go and whom you're with, but so long as you tell us where you're going . . . Oh, bother! I need some cooking apples for the pie.'

'I'll get them,' I offered, taking the bowl from the table. 'About six large ones?'

I ran up the stairs, then went to the end of the landing and climbed the bare wooden staircase to the apple loft. The room ran the full length and width of the house, the ceiling sloping down to the eaves. Strong black beams supporting the roof rose from bare floor-boards and two dormer windows, one at each end, lit the space. The fresh, sharp smell of apples, the spicy scent of drying herbs, mingled with the tang of strings of onions hanging from a ledge, reminding me of when Greg and I used to play up there on wet days.

When I'd selected the apples I crossed to the part of the loft where oddments of broken furniture, battered old trunks and boxes of books were stored beneath the window that looked out across the moors. Here, the light streamed in to pick out the carving on a cradle in which I used to put my dolls to sleep. It wasn't a dolls' cradle, but it was very small, and I'd seen one like it recently in a museum among examples of early Victorian furniture. It hung from a slender but strong wooden frame, and the slightest touch set it rocking.

Mum had mentioned a cradle my father had made for me, 'all carved with leaves and flowers'. I caught my breath and moved closer to examine the cradle. It was shaped like a box, with the sides sloping outwards from the base, and there was a wooden canopy at the head. The carving, which I'd never noticed before, was incredible. It covered the canopy and continued along the edges of the sides. There were tiny flowers and buds and leaves, all intertwining, and when I touched the wood it was silky smooth.

My finger traced the outline of a leaf. My father must have taken ages to carve the intricate design. I tried to imagine him, sitting on the front step at Hawthorn Cottage, absorbed in the work, but the picture wouldn't come because I didn't know what he looked like. I was touching something he had held in his hands and worked on with loving care, yet I could get no closer to him than that.

I set the cradle rocking gently and glanced towards the corner of the room, where there was a child's highchair in matching wood, and a cot that had been painted white.

I stepped over some packing cases to look at the cot. It was quite ordinary and practical, with a drop-down side. The white paint was yellowed now but I could see, on the headboard, a trace of pastel colours. I dragged the cot nearer to the window, where it was clear that a design had been painted on the headboard — a delicate design of elves and fairies, some dancing, some peeping from behind flowers. The colours were faded but the work was exquisite, like the illustrations in an old book of nursery rhymes.

Gran was waiting for the apples, so I pushed the cot back and dashed downstairs.

'Sorry,' I panted, putting the apples on the table. 'I got caught up, looking at the cradle and the cot.'

Gran smiled. 'You used to put your dolls to sleep in

that cradle,' she said. 'I expect it seems a very long time ago, to you.'

Why couldn't she tell me my father had made it?

'Until today,' I said. 'I never noticed the carving on it. Was it my cradle?'

'Yes, and the cot and highchair were yours, too.'

I washed my hands and began to peel the apples. What if I asked who did the carving? No. I couldn't force Gran into that situation. Even now, I could sense a sort of tension in the air – the sort of feeling you get when someone is embarrassed and you try to think of something to say that will rescue them. Maybe I was imagining it, but there'd be another opportunity. I had to let it go.

'Gran,' I said, 'I've been wondering if you could put up with me for another week. I mean, it doesn't matter a bit if it's not convenient . . .'

'Well, of *course* you can stay!' she cried, apparently delighted. 'Provided your mother agrees, of course. She may have something planned for next week.'

'I'm sure she hasn't,' I replied. 'She just didn't think of asking for longer than the time she's in Malta.'

Gran laughed. 'More likely she thought you'd be bored out of your mind, and anxious to get home! We'd love to have you, Sarah, for as long as you want to stay. If you want to come back here after Florida, you'll be more than welcome.'

I hugged her, and went to get the cinnamon for the apple pie from the cupboard. I wished I could tell her I didn't want to go to Florida, but it seemed like being disloyal to Mum.

When the cooking was in the oven, Gran made coffee, and I took some out to the stables for Claire and the other stable girls, Joanna and Kate. After coffee, I helped Claire in the stables, and she said I could have Brandy for the afternoon. 'I can't come with you today,' she said. 'I've got to work with the foals. Soon we'll separate them from the mares, and get them weaned. Today we're going to put bridles on them, and start getting them used to a leading rein.'

'Couldn't I help with that?' I asked eagerly.

'No, Sarah. Thanks, but you do need to be experienced to put them on their first lead. You help a lot already, by going into the paddock with them and handling them.'

I stared at her. 'What? I just stroke them.'

She nodded. 'We have to spare time just to stroke them. They have to get used to being handled. Otherwise, when the vet has to examine them, he can't manage them. They're still wild things, you know. If we don't make them friendly, they'll be of no use to anyone, which means they won't get good homes.'

I was astonished. 'I thought they were naturally friendly!' I exclaimed. 'Most of them come to me, willingly.'

'If the mother's friendly and co-operative,' Claire said, 'they often are friendly, because they copy her. But not always. Every day, we have to run our hands all over them, along their bodies, down their legs, then eventually they don't mind when we put a little light bridle on them. Then we can start training them. Nobody wants a horse you can do nothing with.'

'I'll play with them as much as you like,' I grinned. 'I didn't know I was working! Oh, Claire, I wish we lived in the country! Maybe, if we did, Grandad would give me one of the foals!'

'I expect he would,' she said, 'and when you see Alison's puppies, you'll want one of those. If you lived in the country you'd need three acres of land just to keep your animals on!'

That afternoon, I helped Claire saddle up Brandy and rode her out on to the moors, resisting the temptation to ride round the village to look for the camp site in the hope of seeing Greg. After all, it wasn't likely that he, too, was reliving yesterday, recalling things I'd said, remembering the moment when he'd kissed me.

I'd never felt like this before. I'd had to stop myself from bringing Greg into every conversation. Luckily, I remembered a girl at school, Lucy Carter, who'd fallen in love with the Chemistry master, Mr Stevens. She'd bored us all stiff, talking about him all the time, writing *poetry* about him! I suppose he was quite good-looking in an academic sort of way, with his rather pale, clever face, and glasses, and untidy curly hair, but she drove us all mad. She was *obsessed*. So, when I heard myself at breakfast saying, 'Greg thinks . . .' and five minutes later, 'Greg says . . .' I recognized the Lucy Carter syndrome and shut up.

Now I knew how Lucy had felt. That is, until she saw Mr Stevens in a restaurant, gazing into the eyes of a girl with red hair. From that moment, she hated him. She even stopped bothering with Chemistry just to spite him. And all the time, Mr Stevens never took any more notice of Lucy than he did of anyone else.

It must have been awful for her. I hadn't realized. I just thought she'd gone round the twist. But Mr Stevens was old, and unnattainable. Well – he's about Mum's age, I think. Did Lucy really feel about him the way I felt about Greg?

Today, I missed him terribly. If there hadn't been a million things to do at the farm I'm sure I'd have felt miserable, being apart from him. Pehaps this was love. Could you be in love with someone after only one afternoon and evening in his company?

There was definitely something different about me. I felt more alive. Looking out towards the hills, I noticed all the varying colours of bracken and heather, and the sharp emerald green of the grass on the slopes, which Greg said was due to limestone in the soil. A group of hikers with packs on their backs waved to me and I waved back, and I wanted them to have a really super holiday. I just wanted everyone to feel as happy as I did. And, on top of all that, I was going to stay here for an extra week!

If only I didn't, now and again, remember the black cloud that hung over me – the fear of what I might discover about my father – life would be almost too perfect to bear.

I got back to the farmhouse in time for tea, and after tea I took the dogs out. It was still very hot so I took them to the woods, where they prowled the under-growth, itching to be let off their leads. I set them free and they began stalking imaginary prey and rushing around as if they were after rabbits.

It was cool and quiet in the woods, the air full of the fragrance of the trees and wild flowers. I came to a clearing, where a little stream hurried through, and a weeping willow dipped its branches in the water. I blinked as I came into the sunlight, then stopped quite still. A fawn was drinking at the stream, its long legs splayed apart, its slender neck bent to the water. I hardly breathed as I watched it, but then it sensed the dogs and bounded into cover. A red squirrel dashed, chattering hysterically, up a tree and perched there, watching me warily.

On the banks of the stream there were drifts of white, star-shaped flowers. I sat down surrounded by them, then lay back in the grass, the sun warm on my face, and once again the problem I had to solve took possession of me. I closed my eyes and tried to work out some plan. If I pretended I was researching local history for a school project, could I persuade some of the villagers to talk about unusual things that had happened here, say thirteen years ago?

Aunt Jane had said, 'What happened that night wasn't your fault' — something like that. So it seemed that the night my father died was memorable in some way. The trouble was, if I gave my name, or hinted at my identity, no one would talk to me about him.

The scent of the flowers was sweet and heavy, like the scent of violets. The dogs were crashing around somewhere nearby. I felt myself drifting, as if on a cloud, like in the moment just before sleep. There was another scent mingled with the sweetness of the flowers. It was woodsmoke, so there must be a bonfire somewhere. Even with the burden on my mind, the peace was wonderful.

Then, suddenly, there was a sharp crack, like gun-fire, and I was lifted bodily into the air — snatched up and carried, as if I had no strength to resist. In some way I knew I was dreaming, yet I couldn't force myself awake. I was limp and helpless, as if I'd been drugged. I was being carried through a forest, and it was pitch dark. I felt the branches of trees scratch my bare arms and legs as I was borne along. I tried to scream, but no sound came. A man's voice called out, loud and clear, 'Let her go!', and then something cold and wet was on my face . . .

I sat up, my eyes wide open, to find Bruno licking my face. Boxer, the other dog, was sitting a yard away, looking at me, his tongue lolling, his eyes bright with excitement.

I was trembling as I stared fearfully around, but the clearing was still the same beautiful spot. Relief flooded through me. I must have fallen into a light sleep and had a horrible dream. I'd never in all my life had a nightmare, and if it was like that, I hoped I never would again. I could still feel the awful sensation of being carried along, helpless, by someone immensely strong. I shuddered, and put my arms around Bruno and laid my cheek against his long silky hair. 'Thank you, Bruno,' I gasped. 'Thank you for waking me up. You wouldn't let anyone carry me away, would you?'

He quivered with pleasure and crept close to me. Boxer joined him, not wanting to be left out. Both dogs were competing for attention and I gladly gave it, grateful for their presence which brought me back to earth.

I stood up and gazed around, still shaken by the experience. The sun glinted on the water and the dogs dashed in for a quick paddle in the shallow stream before we continued to the edge of the wood. Soon the scent of woodsmoke which had been in my dream became reality. I could hear the rhythmic sound of an axe attacking a tree trunk. So I hadn't imagined the bonfire. The memory of the dream was still with me. Why on earth should I dream of gunshot, and someone shouting, 'Let her go!', and experience that dreadful sensation of being snatched up and carried off so easily, as if I weighed nothing? Why did I fall asleep, anyway, in daylight, in the late afternoon? Well, maybe that was explainable. I wasn't used to so much physical activity at home, and I was much more relaxed now that the exams were over. I was off-guard, with no pressures to cope with, and I was in tune with nature. And a fat lot of use all that was, if it gave me nightmares!

I could see the bonfire at the edge of the wood now. A man was felling trees and burning the branches. I watched him for a moment from afar and the weird, unearthly experience of the dream vanished, as if by magic. It had needed only the sight of a real man, doing a hard day's work, to bring me back to reality.

After dinner that evening, I went out to fasten up the doors of the henhouse while Grandad did his rounds of the stables. I was checking that there were no hens roosting in the barn, where a fox might get in, when Gran called me to the phone.

It was Mum, calling from Malta. I told her that Gran said I could stay longer if she agreed, and her voice became anxious as she said, 'Now, darling, you don't *have* to stay, out of politeness, just because they've invited you. Tell Gran I've arranged something for next week, which you'd forgotten about. Hang on, let me try to think of something . . .'

'No, Mum, honestly, I *want* to stay. *I* asked Gran if I could stay for next week.'

There was a pause, then an incredulous, 'You *did*? Well, don't blame me if you get tired of it and want to change your mind. If you accept, you'll *have* to stay, even after the novelty's worn off.'

'Mum – I really do want to stay. Thanks for agreeing. How's the conference going? Is the hotel nice?'

'It's superb, and I've met some very interesting people. The evenings are very sociable. I'll tell you all about it when I get back.'

'Super.' I paused, not knowing what to say next. Then I decided to tell her about Greg. 'I've met someone interesting, too. You remember Greg Anderson? He used to come here to play with me every day in the school holidays, years ago. He wasn't here last time, but all the holidays before that – do you remember him?'

'Greg Anderson? Oh! The doctor's son! A dear little chap with blond curls and freckles. Always cheerful. You've met up again? That's nice. Such a friendly little boy.'

'Well, he's a bit different now, Mum. Still friendly and cheerful, but, Mum – he's eighteen!'

'*Eighteen?* Good heavens! Well, yes, I suppose he must be. Do you still get on well with him?'

'Very well, but I'll tell you more about him when I see you. Not that it'll be as exciting as your news.'

'Yes it will. Mine's fifty per cent work. Well – maybe thirty per cent. What's the weather like with you?'

'Blazing sunshine. What's it like in Malta?'

'Scorching! But there's air conditioning in the conference room where we meet every morning. We swim every evening to cool off, then go out somewhere. Are you doing any riding?'

'Yes. Every day so far. Last night I went to a barn dance.'

'What – in Thorndale? They'll be opening a casino

next! Well, darling, I'd better go now.'

'Yes. This must be very expensive. Thanks for ring-ing, Mum.'

I'd just replaced the receiver when the phone rang again, so I picked it up and said, 'Greenacres Farm.'

To my absolute joy, Greg's voice answered, 'Hello, Sarah.'

'Greg! Hi! Did you want Grandad?'

'Now why should I want your grandad?' he laughed. 'No. I've something to tell you. You'd better watch what you say, in case anyone overhears. I met a journ-alist at the camp site today, and he had some advice about how we can find out about your father.'

'Oh, Greg!' I gasped.

'He gave me a few suggestions. Journalists have ways of finding things out. If you're free tomorrow evening, could we meet, and I'll explain?'

'Yes. What time?'

'I'll come at about seven-thirty.'

'Fine. I'll look forward to seeing you. And, Greg – *thanks*.'

'Any problem last night, about getting in late?'

'None at all. I did enjoy it, Greg.'

'So did I. Tonight, I've had to work at the camp site. Every Wednesday I have to check gas containers. Still, I get paid for it, so I'm not complaining. See you tomorrow. 'Bye, Sarah.'

I held the receiver for a moment before replacing it, as if I could hang on to the sound of his voice for a little longer. This really must be how people felt when they were in love. I'd thought it would never happen to me. In fact, I'd wondered if it really happened to anyone at all. Perhaps, I'd thought, it was all made up – for books and songs, exaggerated out of all proportion. Someone at school said Lucy Carter had gone all the way to Highgate on the bus to look at the house where Mr Stevens lived. I'd simply not believed that at all. Now, I wasn't sure . . .

Gran came into the hall, saying, 'I thought I heard the phone ring again.'

'Yes. It was Greg, for me. Is it all right if I go out with him tomorrow evening?'

'Of course,' she nodded. 'Your mother seems to be having a very good time. I thought it was supposed to be a conference. She was telling me about this very unusual night club they all go to.'

I laughed. 'That will be research.'

'Ah, yes,' she said drily. 'I should have realized.'

'Ouch!' I remembered. 'I've left the barn doors open!'

I dashed outside and checked the barn again, then closed the big doors and clicked the padlock shut. Then I leaned against the doors and took a deep breath, still savouring the excitement of having talked to Greg. He must feel something for me, or he wouldn't have thought of my problem when he was talking to the journalist. Or was he just interested in solving a puzzle?

A cat was slinking across the roof of the henhouse. It saw me, jumped down and ran to me with a little cry, rubbing its head around my ankles.

'Hello, cat,' I said. 'You're not one of the house cats. I've not seen you before. Do you live in the stables?' I picked it up and put my cheek against its soft fur. 'Oh, puss,' I whispered, 'do you know what it's like to be really, truly happy?'

The cat began to purr loudly. 'I expect you're happy all the time,' I said wonderingly. It climbed on to my shoulder and rubbed its head against my face, still purring. In the half light I couldn't see what colour it was, though I could tell there was no white on it. But even in the darkness, its eyes glowed a beautiful soft green, like the leaves of trees in early spring.

Suddenly the cat stiffened, spotting a movement on the ground. It jumped down and walked slowly on stiff legs across the yard, its whole body concentrated on a patch of shadow near the shed door.

'You're fickle!' I told it. 'The minute you see something interesting, you're off, without a backward glance!'

Later, as I lay in bed with my bedside light still on, thinking about Greg, wondering what suggestions the journalist had made, there was a scrabbling sound at my window. A pair of pointed ears appeared above the sill. Announcing himself with the familiar little mewing cry, the cat stepped through the open window and leapt lightly on to my bed.

'Hi, cat!' I smiled. 'I'm sorry I called you fickle.' He was black all over and as I stroked his thick fur, he curled up close to me, purring as loudly as ever.

'You're not at all fickle,' I told him, 'and you're a lucky black cat. I wonder if you can work spells? If by any chance you can, there's a boy I'm meeting tomorrow night . . .'

# Chapter 6

As soon as I was in the car beside Greg, on the way to the village the following evening, I told him I was staying for an extra week.

'Great!' he said, and I knew by his quick smile and the way he turned to glance at me that he really was pleased. 'I thought we'd go to the Red Lion for a drink,' he said. 'We can talk there.'

'Oh, Greg,' I sighed. 'I'm sorry. I can't go into pubs.'

'We can go into the gardens,' he said. 'In this weather, they have tables outside.'

'But – you'd rather go inside, wouldn't you?' I murmured.

'No. Not in this heat. Why should I want to go inside?'

'Well, you're old enough.'

He grinned. 'I'm old enough to go to prison, but I don't especially want to! It's noisy in the pub, anyway, and we've got things to discuss.'

Soon we were sitting at a table in the garden of the Red Lion Inn, surrounded by trees, cool and shady. Greg had lager, and I had bitter lemon. I always had that at Mum's parties, because it looks like a real drink and people don't keep pestering you to have something stronger.

Greg told me about the journalist who was camping on the site. He'd asked Greg the way to the church, because he wanted to look up something in the parish register.

'He's tracing his ancestry,' Greg said. 'Combining a holiday with doing the research. I was interested in what he'd done already, so he showed me his notes, and then I suddenly thought he might be able to help us.

'I asked him how he would go about tracking down information about something that happened thirteen years ago, and I had to explain that it was a death: that we wanted to know if it was accidental or suicide, and what circumstances surrounded it.

'He said if it was an accident or suicide, there'd have to be an inquest, and the inquest would be reported in the local paper. He said you can look up back copies of any newspaper. If they haven't got them at the local newspaper office, there's a place in London . . .' Greg took a piece of paper from his pocket and read, 'The Colindale Newspaper Library. They have copies of every newspaper ever printed in England. But he said we should try the local newspaper office first.'

I felt my heart begin to race. 'How many local newspapers are there, here?' I asked.

'Only one,' he replied. 'The offices are in Charnley. That's only about thirty miles away. I thought, if you like, I'd phone them and ask if they keep back copies that old, and if we can go and look at them. You wouldn't want to phone yourself, from the farm, would you?'

'No,' I answered, 'someone might overhear. Do you know which buses go to Charnley, Greg?'

'Well,' he grinned. 'I know my car is old and tatty, but—'

'You mean — you'll take me? You'll help me look through the old newspapers?'

'Of course! I've got Monday afternoon off. I'll try to fix it for then, shall I?'

'It's very good of you. Greg, I've been wondering so many things . . . If we don't find anything, then maybe he didn't die. I mean, maybe there was a shooting accident, but what if he's still alive? I know it's stupid to think like this, but when people won't talk to me . . .'

He nodded. 'I thought of that, too,' he said quietly. 'Not that I think it's likely, but—' he referred to the piece of paper again. 'This guy said you can check births, marriages, and deaths at a place called St Catherine's House, in London. I mean, if there was no death certificate there, then he'd have to be still alive.'

'You thought of it, too?' I gazed at him, amazed.

He frowned. 'You have to think of everything. I just couldn't work out a reason for all the secrecy. I mean, why can't they just tell you about the accident, how it happened, where it happened, and why is there this thing you ought to be told about? That man driving the tractor — why did he suddenly stop talking and drive off?'

'Greg,' I murmured, 'these places in London — I should think you have to be eighteen to be allowed to look anything up. If there's nothing in the newspapers, I don't know how—'

'That's all right,' he said. 'I could come to London for a day. The Inter-City trains are fantastic. We could—'

'You'd actually do that, for me?' I gazed at him in wonder.

'Why not? You need to know.'

'Oh, Greg, it's so good of you,' I whispered, feeling the hot tears prick at the back of my eyes. Without thinking, I reached across the table and touched his hand. He took my hand and gripped it gently. I was looking into his eyes, trying not to let my lip tremble, determined not to cry, and in that moment I realized just how much I loved him. I wanted to tell him, but I didn't dare. And besides, a stupid tear was edging its way down the side of my nose. The really awful thing was that I had to take my hand away from his to get a tissue from my bag! It always annoyed Mum that I was so emotional, and I did wish I could grow out of it. I couldn't imagine Mum having to battle with tears at an inconvenient time!

'Sarah!' Greg murmured softly. 'Oh, Sarah, don't cry! It'll be all right. I'm sure it will. Things always work out. You'll see.'

I nodded dumbly as I dried my eyes and sniffed, 'I'm sorry. I'm not a bit sad. I'm only crying because — because you understand.'

Suddenly a voice called, 'Hey! Look who's here!' Rod and Alison, whom we'd met at the barn dance, were coming to our table.

'When are you coming to see our puppies?' Alison demanded. 'Shall I come over and fetch you? Dad would let me take the Land Rover tomorrow afternoon, I think.'

Greg asked them to join us, and Rod said, 'No! We don't want to gatecrash! We just came to say hello.'

We persuaded them to stay and they put their drinks on our table. I said, 'I could ride over to your farm tomorrow afternoon, Alison. Grandad lets me have one of his mares.'

'Great!' she said. 'Come about four and we'll stop for tea. You can meet Mum and Dad and my brother, Jem, and then we'll show you the farm.'

'She won't want to see the farm,' Rod grinned. 'She can't be into cattle and pigs and sheep.'

'She *is*, though,' Alison told him. 'She's going to be a vet.'

'I wish I felt that confident about it,' I sighed. 'I haven't even done A levels yet. Oh, I nearly forgot, Alison, Claire says she keeps meaning to ask you to come and see the foals. We've got seven fillies and five colts.'

'I want to see the foals, too,' Rod said. 'Ask Claire to ring us and say when it's convenient will you?'

We talked to Rod and Alison for ages. I remembered that I didn't want to risk being out late again. Despite what Gran said, it did mean that she had to leave the front door unbolted, and although people weren't as security-conscious here as we were in London, I didn't want to be a nuisance.

I mentioned this to Greg, and he said, 'Yes, better not push our luck. I'll get a reputation for keeping you out late.'

'The seducer of Thorndale,' Rod grinned. 'Headlines in Sunday papers, " 'Doctor's son was my downfall,' says disgraced student Sarah." '

'But you and Greg don't have to get up early,' Alison sighed enviously. 'You're like the idle rich.'

Greg nearly choked on his drink, and I gasped, 'What? *Us?*'

Rod said, 'For you, Sarah, life won't be so cosy, if you're going to be a vet, but Greg's got it *made*! He'll soon be swanning around at medical school, playing practical jokes, like in those "Doctor" films on television.'

'Those are *comedies*!' Greg protested. '*Swanning around*?'

'When I was your age,' Rod began, and I interrupted with, 'All of two years ago!' 'When I was his age,' Rod repeated, 'for three years, I'd been up at six, no breakfast till milking was over, and—'

'*Listen*!' Greg said suddenly and held up his hand, so that we all listened, but heard nothing unusual. 'Funny,' Greg murmured. 'I could have sworn I heard violins! Rod – how do you think medical students pass exams? I'll be at lectures all day, studying half the night—'

'In an attic,' Alison said, 'with a guttering oil lamp, and no heating, so you have to wrap yourself in old blankets, and you have no money for food. I saw the film. You pawn your microscope in a very good cause, and have to borrow one . . .'

'As for getting up at six,' Greg said to Rod, 'at least you've been to bed. In hospital training, doctors can't count on getting any sleep at all. You can be on call three nights running.'

'So are we, at lambing time,' Alison said. 'For you, Greg, it will be only temporary. Eventually, you can become a consultant, or specialize in something like cosmetic surgery – charge the earth to keep rich women looking beautiful.'

I giggled. 'He wants to be a country GP,' I said. 'He'll probably come back here, as his father's assistant.'

'*What*?' Rod gasped. 'Oh *no*! We'll have to sell up and move!'

'You mean,' Greg said, 'that you're not prepared to put your life in my hands?'

'No way!' Rod exclaimed. 'Why pick on your friends? Like Alison says, be a cosmetic surgeon. You could have everything — a yacht, a Rolls. *Think* about it, Greg, for our sakes.'

Alison added, 'You could marry Sarah, and buy her lots of jewellery. We could come and stay on your yacht.'

'Stay on my yacht, when you don't trust me to treat you?' Greg replied. 'You'll be wanting to drive my Rolls next!'

'My mink coat will get ruined,' I sighed. 'I'll be grubbing about in cow sheds and pigsties.'

Rod said, 'You could get a town practice, Sarah. Treat the spoilt pets of the rich and famous.'

'But I want to live in the country, too,' I grinned. 'Seems Greg and I are hopeless cases. I want to work with farm animals as well as domestic pets.'

Rod nodded, suddenly serious. 'Well, you've got to aim for what suits you. I grumble about my life, but I wouldn't change it. It's what I like doing.'

'Me too,' Alison murmured, and I saw them exchange a warm, secret glance. It was nice. You could tell they were in love. I wondered if Greg and I would ever exchange that sort of look, sending an unspoken message that only we understood.

I did wish Alison hadn't joked about Greg marrying me. She hadn't meant anything, but I still wasn't sure how Greg felt about me, and I was so afraid he might feel trapped and stop seeing me.

As we drove back to the farm, Greg said, 'It's good you're staying another week. I'll be able to get some time off next week. Someone's due back from holiday. I might be able to get a whole day off. We could go to York, or Scarborough.'

'I'd love that, Greg, if you're sure you can spare the time. But you must let me pay half the petrol. Mum gave me quite a lot of money, and there's nothing to spend it on, here, so—'

'Thanks for offering,' he smiled, 'but I'm all right for cash at the moment. I'll let you know if it runs out.'

I sighed suddenly. 'If only I didn't have to go to Florida,' I said.

He laughed. 'Well, that's a remark I've not heard very often!'

I nodded. 'I feel mean, just saying it. I know I ought to be thrilled – or at least grateful.'

'Once you're there,' he said, 'it'll be great. It was just that holiday where you got stuck with the geology freak, wasn't it? You must have enjoyed other holidays.'

I thought about it, then said, 'Not really. New places are always fascinating, but it's the pressure. I feel under an obligation to enjoy myself, to fill every moment with activity of some kind. The truth is, Mum and I have so little in common.'

As I said that, it seemed strange. It was something I'd always known, but never acknowledged before. Here, I was free as I never was at home. No one expected me to conform to any pattern. Still, it had to end some-time, and I'd got a week's reprieve.

We reached the little bridge over the river, and the car's headlights cut through the darkness as we turned into the road that led to the farm. I'd begun to dread parting from Greg. It was weird, wanting to be with someone all the time.

The downstairs lights were still on as the car tyres crunched the gravel of the drive. Greg switched off the engine, took me in his arms and kissed me. 'I'll ring you tomorrow; let you know if the newspaper office agree to our going on Monday,' he murmured.

My arms were around his neck, my cheek against his. 'I'll never be able to thank you enough,' I whispered.

'For what?' he asked softly. 'For enjoying your company? For monopolizing your time?' In the dimness of the car, his eyes were shining.

'I'm grateful for that as well,' I smiled.

We walked hand in hand, up the three steps of the front porch. As Greg put his arms around me and kissed me again I wished time would stand still, and that we didn't have to part.

'I'd better go,' he murmured, 'before your grandad comes out with his shotgun!'

As I went into the house, Gran called, 'Had a nice time, Sarah?'

'Super,' I answered, going towards the sitting room. 'We met Rod and Alison. Alison's asked me to go and see her puppies tomorrow afternoon. Grandad, shall I lock up?'

Grandad put his book aside and got up from his armchair. 'I'll do it,' he said. 'Don't go falling in love with those puppies, now! A London flat is no place for a border collie.'

I sat on the arm of the sofa, leaning across to see what Gran was knitting. 'I know, Grandad,' I smiled. 'I know I can't have any pets.'

He turned back from the door and came to put his arm around me. 'Never mind, love,' he muttered. 'You will, one day. When you've finished your education, you'll be able to have the things you want.'

I looked up at him, surprised. I hadn't realized that he understood how I longed for a cat or a dog — something to love and care for. I put my arms around his waist and hugged him.

'You've got advantages, Sarah,' he said gruffly. 'The thing to do is make the most of them. Keep at your school work. That's your passport to getting where you want to be. Do you know what I mean?'

'Yes, Grandad. I think so.'

'That's right,' he said, and patted my shoulder and went into the hall to lock and bolt the door.

I slid down on to the sofa, and picked up the knitting pattern Gran was working from. 'It's just like that polo-neck sweater we were looking at in that magazine yesterday,' I said.

She nodded. 'You said you liked it. Is the colour all right?'

The wool was scarlet — a really sizzling scarlet. 'Fantastic! Do you mean it's for *me*?'

'I doubt if I'll be able to finish it before you go home, though. I'll have to post it to you.'

'Oh, Gran! It's going to be really super! Why is everyone so kind to me?'

I heard Grandad's voice answer me from the doorway. 'I'm going to be very unkind to you now. Brutal, in fact!'

I pretended to cower down into the cushions of the sofa, and covered my head with my hands. 'No, please,

Grandad!' I begged. 'Don't be brutal! What have I done wrong? I'm sorry! I'm sorry! I'll never do it again!'

'I saw you riding without a hard hat this afternoon,' he said. 'I gave you strict instructions. I feel so strongly about it that I won't let you have Brandy again unless you promise me—'

'But – I *did* wear one, Grandad!' I emerged from the cushions, to stare at him blankly. 'Oh – I remember now! I had to go back for it. I forgot it. But I'd only got to the gate when I remembered and went back.'

'That's all right then,' he nodded. 'But always remember, Sarah, it's a rule here. You'll never see Claire riding without one, and she's an experienced horsewoman. I wear one myself. I suppose you've borrowed one. Does it fit properly?'

'Yes. It's my size. It's Joanna's spare one.'

'Well, I'm going into Kirkfield tomorrow morning. You'd better come with me and we'll get you one of your own, and some jodhpurs. It's not comfortable, riding in jeans.'

'But, Grandad, I'll only be here for another week! Riding kit is so expensive!'

'You are going to have a proper kit of your own,' he insisted. 'I'll talk to your mother about arranging some riding for you at home, so the kit won't be wasted.'

'It's ever so expensive, riding in London,' I gasped.

'Everything's expensive in London,' he replied. 'You'd like to be able to go riding at home, wouldn't you?'

'I'd love it, but I don't know if Mum will agree,' I answered.

'I don't suppose you've ever asked her,' Gran said.

'It's like the music lessons.'

'What music lessons?' I asked, baffled.

'When you were little, about six or seven years old, you'd spend hours at the old piano in the dining room, here. You could pick out several tunes, too. Do you remember?'

I laughed. 'Oh yes! I used to keep on at Mum to get a piano, but there wasn't room in the flat.'

Gran said, 'And when you moved to a bigger flat, you still couldn't have one, because the neighbours would have complained about your practising.'

'Yes, they would,' I agreed. 'This is the first flat we've had that's really soundproof.'

Grandad murmured, 'But you still haven't got a piano.'

'No. Mum's got all the furniture arranged just as she wants it. A piano wouldn't fit in.' I turned to Gran. 'What did you mean about music lessons? I've never had any.'

'That's what I mean,' she replied. 'Other girls at your school have music lessons, and surely a lot of them live in flats?'

I frowned. 'Yes, they do. There's a practice room at school which they can use. Actually, I've always wanted to learn to play the violin. Still,' I sighed. 'It's too late now.'

'I don't think it would be too late, for *you*,' Gran murmured. 'He used to play the violin, and he'd never had a lesson in his life. He could play the flute too. It was so beautiful to listen to, wasn't it, John?'

Grandad gave her a sharp look, and then said, 'It was. Yes – beautiful. It certainly was.'

I glanced from one to the other, hardly believing what I'd heard, and remembering what the man on the tractor had said: 'He could play the violin fit to tear your heart out.' 'Who?' I gasped. 'Who used to do that?' I knew they must be talking about my father, but I wanted to hear someone say it aloud.

'Why – Jack,' Gran said. 'Your father. Didn't you know?'

'Look at the time!' Grandad said suddenly. 'I'll be walking about like a zombie tomorrow! Sarah – up bright and early for you! We're going into Kirkfield.'

Gran gathered up her knitting. 'No need for Sarah to get up that early,' she murmured. 'The shops don't open till nine.'

Later, I lay in bed, still stunned at what had happened. If Gran and Grandad had severed all relations with Mum and my father, when had they heard him play the violin, or the flute?

Obviously, Gran hadn't meant to mention him. Momentarily, she'd forgotten whatever pact had been made never to speak about my father in front of me, and Grandad had glossed it over as best he could. Did this mean I could ask about him? I closed my eyes tight in the effort it took to recall just how Gran had spoken – her tone of voice, and the words she'd used. There had been no bitterness. Yet she hadn't meant to speak of him, and Grandad had shot her a warning look.

After the weekend, I might know the answer to all this. I shivered with apprehension. On Monday, all the anxiety, all the doubts and fears might be over, and I'd understand everything, perhaps. Meantime, I didn't want to risk spoiling the atmosphere here. I supposed I could wait until Monday. But if nothing came of our search through the old newspapers, then I'd have to ask Gran and Grandad to tell me the truth, and take the consequences.

# Chapter 7

Next morning in Kirkfield I met Claire's fiancé, Philip, who was the local saddler. Grandad took some saddlery to him for repair, and introduced me to the tall, muscular young man with thick fair hair and a broad pleasant face. I thought how well suited he and Claire were.

Grandad left me in the riding outfitters', to try on hats and jodhpurs and jackets, while he went to collect some tools he'd ordered, telling the owner of the shop to put my purchases on his account and to find me some boots, too.

I dreaded to think of the price of everything! I really didn't mind riding in jeans and a borrowed hat, but Grandad was adamant.

Still, the jodhpurs were very comfortable, and it would be much better to ride in boots. I slipped on the tweed jacket, which fitted perfectly. 'Might have been made for you, Miss,' the proprietor said. He was an old man with silver hair, pink cheeks and a cheery smile.

While he was wrapping up the parcels, I looked at his display of brooches and pins and found a gold pin in the shape of a riding crop, with a small horseshoe in the centre. 'Do you think my grandfather will like this?' I asked the man, 'or will he think it silly? I mean, he never wears any rings or anything, does he?'

'Good gracious me, Miss,' he said. 'I'm quite sure he

won't think it silly. That is a very discreet pin that any gentleman might wear, say on a cravat, and I have seen your grandfather wearing a cravat. But I'm afraid it is quite expensive.'

'That's okay,' I said, knowing Mum had given me plenty of spending money. 'I want something for my grandmother, too, but I can't see anything suitable.'

'We are rather confined,' he said, 'to items to do with horses. Sporting prints, perhaps, or these, made by a local silversmith. Brooches, as you see, of game birds. Here is a pheasant, and there are many other birds.'

He placed a tray on the counter, displaying silver brooches in delicate filigree work. I picked up a cockerel with tiny amethyst eyes and tail feathers of silver, thin as hairs, spangled with tiny stones that glittered red and gold.

'The craftsman makes them from silver left over from his commissioned work,' the man said. 'More for pleasure than profit. It isn't paste jewellery, but semi-precious stones too small to use for rings. Garnets, amber, and so on.'

'I've never seen anything so small and pretty,' I said. 'Gran will love this cockerel.' I would have liked to buy one for Mum, but I just knew that none of these birds would go with the kind of clothes she wore. Mum and I didn't like the same sorts of things, anyway.

I had to dash to the Land Rover, in case Grandad was waiting for me, but he wasn't. I went into the general store, which sold everything and did repairs. They couldn't mend my watch strap but fitted a new one there and then. With my watch safely round my wrist again, I called at the post office for some stamps and postcards to send to schoolfriends. I bought one for Lucy Carter. She's not a special friend of mine, and normally I wouldn't have bothered, but now I knew how she must have felt about Mr Stevens I was ashamed of the way I'd thought she was stupid.

While I was waiting by the Land Rover I glanced idly across the road and, with a sudden rush of joy, recognized Greg's Mini, parked at the kerb! He must be here, somewhere! Grabbing my parcels, which I'd dumped on the pavement, I crossed the road to look for him in the shops.

I didn't find him, so I crossed back and was scanning the street for him when I noticed a couple walking up from the station. The girl was fair and very pretty, and her arm was linked through the boy's. She wore a green sleeveless dress with white sandals, and she had a lovely golden suntan. The boy was carrying a suitcase, and they were both laughing. My mouth went dry. The boy was Greg!

I dodged behind the Land Rover and watched them through the side windows, transfixed, as Greg put her case in the boot and opened the passenger door for her. They drove off and I stared after the car, feeling cold all over.

On the way back, Grandad remarked that I was very quiet and I felt awful, after he'd bought me all the riding kit, so I made a tremendous effort, laughed lightly and said, 'Sorry – I was thinking.'

'Ah! Takes it out of you, thinking,' he smiled.

'I've got out of the habit,' I grinned. 'Now that the exams are over.'

I forced myself to appear cheerful, but it wasn't easy. It was as if a light had gone out inside me and, though the day was hot, I still felt cold. Lucy Carter must have felt like this when she found Mr Stevens with the red-haired girl. Once again I was glad of Mum's tuition in keeping up conversations, because all I could think of was Greg and the fair-haired girl.

To add to my misery, when I went into the house Gran handed me a letter – from Peter! I groaned inwardly as I read the last bit: 'I'm counting the days, and soon I'll be counting the hours, until Sunday, when I can hold you in my arms again.'

I wasn't going back on Sunday, and I was never going back to him! Now I'd have to write and tell him I was staying for another week, and also – what? That I'd met another boy? After Greg, I couldn't go back to Peter. But how could I tell him? It seemed so unfair, yet it would also be unfair not to let him look for someone else.

I'd have to write *today*, and I'd never written that sort of letter before. If only Mum was here – she'd know how to do it. I could ask Gran to help me, but she didn't know the situation with Peter, or even how I felt about Greg. But Claire did. I'd told her everything. I'd ask Claire.

We were clearing up the tack room when I asked her.

'Best thing,' she said, 'is to say that, being away from him, you've come to see things objectively and realized you're the wrong type for him.'

'Who isn't?' I muttered. 'Can't be many girls who like wondering why he's suddenly gone into a mood.'

'How can I concentrate, with you muttering?' Claire demanded. 'After finding out you're the wrong type for him,' she went on, 'run yourself down a bit. Like, say he'd be better off with someone who shares his interests.'

I lifted a saddle back on to the rail. 'He'll be lucky!' I murmured. 'Where's he going to find a girl who likes all of them? Brass rubbing, architecture, sports cars, trad jazz, politics—'

'Shut up!' Claire shouted. 'I was just getting into my stride! Do you want my help or not?'

'Sorry,' I said. 'I'm listening, now.'

'Right. Are you interested in architecture?'

'I like old buildings, castles, Tudor houses, imagining how people used to live in them, and—'

'That's not architecture. Architecture is the shape of a building's window, the stone it's built with, and all that. Tell him he ought to have a girl who can take a real interest in what is going to be his future career. Then say the problem is much more basic.'

'Well, it is.'

'Of *course* it is, you clot! But you've got to say so, otherwise he'll argue and say it's all right, you'll get to like architecture. You've got to be definite, see?'

'Yes. How?'

'Well, you keep putting me off, don't you? You finish up saying how much you've enjoyed your time together, and you know he'll understand, now it's over.'

'But he won't. He'll hit the roof!'

Claire sighed. 'Do you want my help or not?'

'Yes, I do. Sorry. I wish I'd brought a pen and paper.'

'On the desk in the corner, under those files.'

On the desk I found a notepad and a Biro. We worked out a letter which made me sound pathetically inadequate for anyone as brilliant as Peter, finishing with the bit about my decision to set him free to find someone who'd appreciate him!

'I wish,' I sighed, 'that I could just tell the truth.'

'Right,' Claire said. 'Scrub all that. Tell him you never did like him much, but, because he's potty about you, and has a car, it suited you to put up with him for the sake of convenience. Now you've met someone you really like a lot, so he can go and jump in the nearest lake.'

'Ouch!' I winced. 'Doesn't the truth sound horrible?'

'Because it *is* horrible,' she replied. 'So you have to write a lot of rubbish. Only you've got to be careful, because anyone as conceited as him will end up thinking you just want him to appreciate you more.'

I looked at the notes I'd made. 'So I finish this by saying that I've enjoyed the happy times, but now I want him to look for another girl, because I shan't be going out with him any more.'

Claire gasped. '*What?* I never said *that*! I put it much more subtly!'

'Yes, but I've got to finish it this way, because he thinks he owns me.'

Claire gave a kind of snort. 'You never ought to have let it get like that, Sarah! Watch it, next time!'

I folded the piece of paper and put it into the pocket of my jeans. 'I might not get the chance to watch it, next time,' I sighed. Then I told her about seeing Greg with the girl in the green dress.

She put down the pile of book-keeping binders she was about to replace on the shelf and turned right round to look at me. '*Sarah!* That could have been *anybody*! Greg's a nice, friendly guy, outgoing and cheerful! He'd take *my* arm if we met at the station, and we'd probably have a good laugh, too!'

'Do you think it could have been just a friend, Claire?'

'How should *I* know? If you'd had the sense you were born with, you'd have crossed the road and spoken to him, instead of hiding. Then you'd know, wouldn't you?'

'It was such a shock,' I muttered. 'I couldn't face him.'

'You could do with a bit less imagination,' she said, putting the binders on the shelf. 'If Greg had a regular girlfriend, I reckon he'd have mentioned her by now. It couldn't have been Mary Sheldrake, because she's tall, with auburn hair. Anyway, her family moved to Norfolk.'

I looked up sharply. 'Who's Mary Sheldrake?'

'Doctor's daughter, from Oakbrook. Her dad and Greg's dad were friends, and Mary went to boarding school, like Greg. In the holidays they used to go about together, take a boat on the river, or go riding. She was a bit older than Greg. They were just friends.'

She glanced at me and said, 'Well – *you* had a boyfriend, didn't you? Greg and Mary both wanted company during the holidays, I expect; no local friends because of both being away at school.'

Now I was jealous of Mary Sheldrake, whom I'd never met!

But surely Claire was right, and Greg would have told me if he had a girlfriend? But I hadn't told him about Peter, had I? What if, on Monday, I found I was keeping him from his girlfriend? Well, in fact, I wouldn't. If that was the case, I'd go to Charnley on the bus, by myself.

Being in love was so awful! So many things could hurt you!

I'd got halfway through writing the letter to Peter on proper stationery when Gran wanted the dining table for lunch, so I left it and helped her serve the meal.

After lunch, I put two small packages on the coffee tray, and Gran said, 'Oh, John, look! These are addressed to us! Sarah! I hope you haven't been buying presents for us!'

'Why not?' I smiled. 'Why should you two have all the fun?'

I was a bit anxious, though. Mum always went on about my taste in things, so that I was never confident about what I bought – especially for other people.

When Gran looked up from opening her present, I was amazed to see that there were tears in her eyes. 'Oh, Sarah! It's so pretty! John, do look at the tiny claws on the cockerel! But it must have been so expensive!'

Grandad was equally pleased with his pin. That was a relief!

'I'm not going to risk losing this in the stables,' he said, putting it in his pocket. 'It will bring me luck, I know it will. Thank you, Buttons!' He kissed the top of my head. He hadn't called me 'Buttons' for years!

It was time to go upstairs and put on my new riding kit, to show them how well everything fitted. I was coming down the stairs in my new outfit, pretending to be a fashion model, with Gran and Grandad laughing in the hall as I paused to strike a pose, when the phone rang.

It was Greg, to tell me that he'd arranged with the *Charnley and District Argus* for us to look at their back copies on Monday afternoon.

'Marvellous,' I said. 'But if you can't spare the time, I can easily go by myself on the bus.'

'No way!' he said. 'I'm free till seven-thirty on Monday, but I have to go back to the camp site for the evening, because a lot of campers arrive then.'

'I just don't want to take up all your free time,' I said anxiously, thinking of the girl in the green dress.

He laughed. 'That's not quite the way I see it! Sarah — are you doing anything exciting tonight? If not, I wondered if you'd like to come here. Dad's on call, but he's at a meeting at the hospital, so I have to be here to relay any emergency calls. We could play records, watch television. If you'd rather stay home and muck out the stables, I wouldn't blame you.'

'I'd love to come,' I gasped. 'What time?'

'Seven? Trouble is, I can't leave the phone after six, so I can't come for you. Would your grandad bring you? I can take you home afterwards, when Dad gets back.'

'It's not far to the village,' I said. 'I'll walk.'

He gave me directions to his house, and I put down the phone. Suddenly, life was wonderful again! But — perhaps his girlfriend wasn't free tonight? No! I wouldn't think about that. Everything was great!

In the afternoon, I rode Brandy over to Alison's house and met her parents and her brother Jem, who's the same age as me — a red-haired boy with freckles; the sort of boy you like straight away. The puppies were wonderful. Jem and Alison showed me over the whole farm, and I rode Brandy back to Greenacres with just enough time to unsaddle her before supper, as they call dinner in Yorkshire.

After supper, I had a shower and put on my pink flowered dress and pink sandals. As I checked my reflection in the long mirror, I imagined Mum's voice saying, 'What about a floppy pink ribbon in your hair, dear, to complete the "country-girl" look?' For a second or two I hesitated, thinking of changing into my blue linen with the white trimming. But I felt right in this dress. I felt comfortable. I wanted to please Greg, not Mum. Most of all, I wanted to feel relaxed, not dressed up.

Greg had said, 'It's the gloomy-looking old house at the end of the High Street.' And it was! Peter would have dated it instantly. 'Early Victorian,' he'd have said. 'Rather a monstrosity.' Something like that. I rang the bell under the brass plate that said, 'Robert Anderson, MD'.

Greg took me through a large, bare hall into a small cosy sitting room full of old-fashioned furniture and shelves crammed with books. On the hearth of the big marble fireplace was a copper container full of red roses. The scent was heavenly. I knelt on the hearthrug to look closely at them, and Greg said, 'Dad's other hobby. Golf and roses. We have a large garden at the back, and roses are his speciality. I'll cut some for you to take home.'

We made coffee in the kitchen that was very like the farmhouse kitchen, and almost as big, with tiled floor and oak cupboards. As we went back into the sitting room, Greg, carrying the tray, I said, 'I saw you in Kirkfield this morning.'

'What? Where were you? Why didn't you yell?'

'Outside the post office. You were just driving off.'

Well, I couldn't say I'd hidden behind the Land Rover!

'I'm sorry we missed each other! I had to meet Madeleine at the station. She's the daughter of the camp site owner, just back from holiday in Tenerife, thank goodness! Now I can have more time off.'

The relief made me almost light-headed.

Strangely, when I looked through Greg's records I found I'd got most of the same albums at home. We listened to music for a while, then went into the garden, where Greg cut me a huge bunch of roses.

The French windows were wide open, so we'd have heard the phone in case there was a call for Dr Anderson, but luckily it didn't ring all evening.

Greg brought out two garden chairs and we sat on the stone patio to enjoy the mild summer evening. The garden had a large lawn surrounded by low-growing shrubs, and behind the shrubs were roses of every type and colour. Tall trees grew all around the boundary of the garden, making it a very private place.

I described the communal gardens at our block of flats. 'Formally laid out,' I said, 'but there are trees, and seats where you can sit in the shade, or you can sunbathe on the grass. It must be lovely to have a big garden like this, all to yourselves.'

'It's a lot of work,' Greg said. 'I get roped in for weeding and mowing the lawn.'

His father came home when we were looking at

some photos Greg had taken in Austria on his last school holiday. I'd expected Dr Anderson to be about Mum's age, but he was older. With greying hair, and blue eyes like Greg's, he was tall and slim and looked nearer Grandad's age than Mum's.

I talked to him while Greg made more coffee. He seemed surprised that I was interested in his roses, and showed me a book with pictures of his favourites. As he talked, I realized that I was doing what Mum had taught me to do in conversation — lean slightly forward, look straight at the person you're talking to, and listen carefully so you can ask sensible questions. And I wasn't even trying! If only Mum's guests talked about interesting things like this, I thought, I'd never need to remember any rules.

As we were leaving, Greg's father lent me a book about gardens; not great and famous places, but private gardens belonging to people who'd made something special out of an ordinary plot.

The lights were still on as we drove up to the farm-house. Greg didn't want to come in, as he had to be at the camp site early next morning. On the porch, he drew me close and kissed me. I touched the soft hair at the back of his neck and felt the familiar warm stirring sensation inside me. If only he would say he loved me! Surely, soon . . . I longed to tell him how I felt about him, but something warned me to wait.

We heard a footstep in the hall and sprang apart. The door opened with quite a lot of fumbling with the latch, and Gran said, 'Greg, I heard your car, and as you don't seem to be coming in—'

Greg told her about having to be up very early, and she said, 'I wondered if you'd like to come to supper tomorrow evening?'

'Thank you, I'd love to,' he answered. 'I finish at five on Saturdays.'

'Well then, come straight here, if you like,' said Gran. 'We'll look forward to seeing you.'

She retreated tactfully inside, but she could hardly close the door again, so we kissed briefly and said good night.

Later, in bed, I was reading the book Greg's father had lent me, and imagining what sort of garden I'd have one day. It seemed I was beginning to live for the future. One day, I'd live in the country, and have a dog and a cat. One day, I'd have a garden . . . I'd never thought about the future before. It had always seemed unreal – another place. Grandad had said that keeping at my school work now was a passport to getting the sort of life I wanted, later.

It was as if 'now' didn't matter. 'Now' was just the time when you laid plans for the future. It didn't seem right. What was wrong with 'now', and why did the future suddenly seem so attractive?

It was being here that had made me think differently. I didn't really understand Mum's job, or even why it was necessary, but I understood what Grandad and Claire and Alison and everyone here was doing, and why they were doing it. Best of all, I never seemed to get things wrong, here. Here, people approved of me. I fitted in. It was a nice, comfortable feeling, but it had made me realize how different life was at home. From this distance, it seemed sort of empty.

I was deep into this self-analysis when the cat jumped on my bed. I'd discovered that his name was Traddles, he lived in the stables and was a close friend of Victor, the big stallion. I hadn't known that horses often have animal friends whom they depend on. Claire told me that Victor wouldn't settle in his stable if Traddles wasn't there. Lately the cat had been visiting me when I went to sleep, but he was always gone in the morning, so I assumed he never left Victor for long.

I told Traddles that Greg was coming to supper tomorrow evening, and he purred and rubbed his head against my chin.

'And on Monday,' I whispered, 'we're going to Charnley, to find out about my father.'

Now that it was so close, I was afraid. I'd never been as happy as I was now, and I didn't want to risk spoiling everything. But it was too late to back out. It was all arranged, for better or worse.

## Chapter 8

On Saturday morning I helped Gran with the cooking, and when Grandad came in for coffee I showed him the book Greg's father had lent me.

Ten minutes later, he was still immersed in it. Gran said, 'Sarah, you must never give Grandad a book to look at during the daytime. He'll not be able to put it down, and the work won't get done.'

'Oh!' I remembered suddenly, 'Dr Anderson said

you might like to have some cuttings of his roses later in the season, whatever that means.'

'That's very kind of him,' said Gran.

Grandad answered, 'It means he'll cut a bit of the stem off, below a bud, so we can plant it and a new rose will grow from it.'

'Oh!' I replied. 'I didn't know that.'

'How could you?' Gran said. 'You've never done any gardening.'

'Don't start on the garden here, Sarah,' Grandad warned. 'What with helping in the stables, feeding the hens, collecting eggs, and helping your gran with the cooking, you'll have no free time at all. I ought to put you on the payroll.'

When he'd gone back to work, Gran said, 'He's going to miss you when you go home. He was wondering last night if you'd like to come back, after Florida. I told him that once you got home you wouldn't want to leave all your friends again, and all the excitement of London.'

I looked up from the book about gardens. 'Oh, Gran! Could I really come back, after Florida? I'd actually rather stay here than go to Florida, in fact.'

'What?' she gasped. 'Sarah, you'd regret making a decision like that! But of course, if your mother agrees, you can come after your holiday.'

'I know she'll agree. Oh, thank you, Gran.'

'You may get tired of being here,' she warned.

'I'll *never* get tired of being here,' I replied. 'I feel as if I *belong* here.'

She smiled. 'When you were little, you used to cry when the holidays were over and you had to go home.'

'Yes. I remember,' I said. 'Gran, just supposing that

Mum doesn't mind if I don't go to Florida, would you let me stay here, instead?'

She looked worried now. 'Sarah, you can stay here whenever you like, for as long as you like. You *do* belong here, when your mother can spare you. But it would be very hurtful to Sally to say that you don't want to go on a wonderful holiday she's arranged for you.'

I sighed. 'But – if it should turn out that she really doesn't mind?'

Doubtfully, Gran said, 'You ought not to miss the chance of going to America, Sarah. You'd regret it, later. And I'm sure Sally *would* mind.'

I helped Claire in the stables until lunchtime, then, after lunch, I set out on Brandy, headed towards the moors, along the familiar track I'd taken each day since I arrived here.

I'd put on my new riding jacket because there was a slight chill in the air, and after I'd been riding for about an hour, a faint mist appeared at ground level, swirling about like a thin veil. Well, the weather *had* been too good to be true, and anyway it was time to set off on the track that led down through the wooded valley and home.

The trouble was, I couldn't see the track for the mist, which seemed to be rising. I couldn't even see Brandy's hooves now. The valley looked clear, though, and I set off in that general direction. I'd seen this sort of mist before, on Bodmin Moor in Cornwall. We'd been in Mum's car, and kept driving out of it, then finding another pocket further along. When the mist cleared, I'd be able to find the track again.

As I rode down the hill the mist crept higher, and seemed to be billowing out from the moor in clouds. I began to feel uneasy. Soon, it was as if Brandy was wading through a bath of steam, only the steam was cold and damp, with an acrid smell. I could see it now, in the valley, drifting in rolling masses across the fields. It was scary, as if it would get higher and higher, and suffocate us.

Grandad had gone on at me about always sticking to paths and tracks, because even people who knew the moors well could get lost, even in good weather. But there were no tracks to be seen. I couldn't even be sure if I was going in the right direction, because the valley was hazy now, and soon it might disappear in the fog. Panic gripped me as I thought of being stranded here.

I reined Brandy in, so I could think what to do. It was cold, not moving, and she gave a little snort of impatience. I couldn't even make out the shape of a bush, or a tree, and still the mist was rising, thickening. Brandy made to move forward, and I checked her. I shivered as I muttered, 'Hang on, Brandy. I've got to work this out.'

We could go blundering on, aiming to reach the valley, then the village, hoping the mist would clear. But part of the way home was beside the river, and I wouldn't be able to see the river when we got to it. Brandy might plunge into the water!

Stories I'd heard about people lost on the moors began to crowd into my mind – people lost for days; people found suffering from exposure. Then I remembered something Grandad had told me, years ago. When he was a boy out riding on the moors, he'd lost his bearings, and darkness had fallen while he was still searching for a familiar landmark. He'd slackened the reins and the horse had taken him home.

But was it a specially intelligent horse, or one used to going the same way so often that it was programmed to find its way back? Could all horses find their way home? Even in fog, or darkness? Well, I had nothing to lose, had I?

I leaned forward and talked to Brandy. 'I'm just going to sit here and let you take over,' I told her. 'If you make a mess of it, it can't be helped. I want you to go home, Brandy. *Home*. Go home, Brandy.'

I let the reins lie slack, and touched her with my heels. She set off purposefully, at a good pace, so that hope leapt inside me. She kept up the brisk, confident stride for perhaps half an hour. I couldn't see my watch to check the time. The damp fog had closed in completely now, wrapping itself around us like a loose bandage. I was shivering with cold and fear.

I heard a sound like the clink of metal, and the mare seemed to be walking differently. We were on a firm surface — a road! The dull, rhythmic thud of hooves had changed to a harder, clipping sound, and she was moving faster. But which road could this be? What if there were cars? Would I see headlights, or any light, through this grey wall that surrounded us? I strained my eyes, which were stinging, irritated by the fog.

Instinct told me that Brandy was moving too fast; that I ought to rein her in; but she'd found the road. Her instinct must be better than mine. I listened, hopeful that I might hear a human voice. Surely, on a road, we were safer? There might be houses nearby, but I couldn't see anything. I'd never known fog could be like this. Pitch darkness was better than fog. You could see lights through darkness. You could see stars.

It must have been about five minutes later that I began to think the fog was thinning a little – or was I just getting more used to it? Then I thought I could see a sort of golden glow ahead of us. I took the reins. This could be a car with headlights on. I slowed Brandy to a sedate walk, just in case, though I was fairly sure no car would be moving. The glow separated into several smaller glows. They were lights! They seemed to hang, suspended in the air, like fuzzy yellow balls. The vague outline of what might be a hedge hovered beside us, and then there was the bulky shape of a building, surrounded by these blurred yellow blobs.

It was a roadside inn, with all its lights on! The relief was indescribable! I slid from the mare and led her into the forecourt and up to the front entrance. I put my arms around her neck, tears of relief and gratitude streaming from my eyes. 'Just wait here a while,' I sniffed. 'I'll ring the farm and we'll soon be home.' I threw her reins over the railings and went into the building.

A short, thickset man came towards me, his face bronzed, his hair greying at the front. He was smiling until he saw that I was shaking with cold.

'Why, you've been caught out in this fog!' he exclaimed. 'You must be frozen through. Come into the lounge. I lit a fire when this mist started. The Green Dragon doesn't open for two hours, but I thought I'd get the place nice and cosy. Take off your damp jacket. Your horse in the yard, is it?'

'No. I left her near the front door. Will you let me make a phone call, please? It's to Greenacres Farm, near Thorndale. Maybe you could tell me how to get back there?'

He ushered me into a warm, comfortable lounge, where a log fire crackled. 'Greenacres is nobbut a couple of miles off,' he said. 'I reckon it'll be clear as day over there. The mist is rolling back now, towards the moors. You sit near the fire. I'll bring a blanket. There's a phone on the bar, there. I'll see to your horse, then I'll make us some coffee.'

I crept close to the fire. Never before had I been so grateful for warmth and the sound of a human voice. Through the window I could see the mist literally rolling away, in great swirling clouds.

My fingers were numb as I dialled the farm number.

'Sarah!' said Gran's voice. 'Where are you? Are you all right?'

I explained what had happened, and she told me that there was no fog at all around the farm. 'We only knew about it when the man delivering feed for the hens told us. He'd narrowly missed getting caught in it. Grandad and Claire have saddled up to come looking for you, but I'll get Grandad to pick you up in the Land Rover. He can bring Claire or Joanna with him to ride Brandy back.'

'*I* can ride Brandy back!' I said. 'I'm all right. Really.'

'But you've had a bad experience—'

'And it's over, and the landlord here is making coffee when he's finished attending to Brandy. Gran, I'm fine, and I'll be home soon. I'll just stay and have coffee and get warm.'

'Well, if you're certain . . .'

'I'm positive, Gran. I'll see you soon.'

'Don't forget Greg's coming to supper, then, and give our regards to Harry. He's the landlord of the Green Dragon. You'll be quite safe with Harry.'

As I put the phone down, the landlord came in with a pink blanket, which he draped around me. 'I've put your jacket to dry off in the kitchen,' he said, 'and my cellarman is seeing to your mare. I'll just go and get the coffee.'

'Thank you, Mr . . .?'

'Call me Harry,' he smiled, and went out. I pulled the soft blanket close around me and held out my hands to the fire.

Harry returned with two steaming mugs of coffee. 'I expect you didn't notice the mist till you were in the middle of it?' he said.

'I saw some sort of milky, cloudy patches on the ground, quite a way off,' I said. 'I didn't think anything of it.'

'Ah! If you knew these moors, love, you'd 'ave taken notice. Still, no harm done. How did you find your way here?'

'I didn't. I just left it to the mare. I wonder if she'd have taken me right to the farm? Do all horses know their way home?'

'You'd 'ave to ask John, your grandad, that, love. I don't know much about horses.'

I sipped the hot coffee gratefully. 'Do you know my grandad well, Harry?' I asked.

'Aye! Known John for years! When you said you were staying at Greenacres, it clicked who you were, all of a sudden. Ever since you stepped through the door, frozen stiff, I'd been wondering who you reminded me of. You're the spitting image of your father!'

I put down my mug, my hands unsteady, and looked at Harry half fearfully, half with hope brimming inside me. But this time, I must be careful. I couldn't bear it if the door was slammed in my face again. Quietly, I said, 'You knew my father?'

'*Knew* him? Aye, I knew him! I'll never forget Jack Leigh. He helped me through a very difficult time. No one else could have done what Jack did.'

He settled himself on the leather chesterfield beside me. 'I was in the Merchant Navy,' he said, 'when my wife died, and my son, Davy, was only ten years old. I came ashore – resigned from the service – and bought this pub, so I could look after Davy. I didn't want a job where I had to leave him with other people all day, not when he'd lost his mother, and was broken-hearted and lonely.

'But, you see, he hardly knew me. All his life I'd only been home on leave, then off to sea again, so he was close to his mother, but I was like a stranger to him. I didn't know how to help him.

'But Jack did. He took Davy fishing, taught him how to build fires in the open, how to recognize different sorts of birds. Did you know that Jack could make bird calls, and birds would come to him? Wild birds, like robins, would perch on his finger. Oh, but you'll have been told all this, many a time!'

Softly, fearfully, I whispered, 'No, Harry. No one talks about him to me. I've always wanted to know about him, but no one will tell me anything.'

He nodded, his expression grave. 'When you've known someone like Jack,' he said, 'it's a bitter thing, to have to accept the loss of him. I can understand your family not being able to talk about him, not wanting to revive sad memories.'

I gazed at him, wondering how he could put that interpretation on it. I wanted him to go on talking about my father. 'I think my grandparents were against the marriage,' I prodded.

'Oh? Well, Jack and Sally would be very young when they got married. I expect they wanted them to wait. I don't know nothing about that because I only came to the Green Dragon fourteen years ago. You'd be about two years old. Jack idolized you! He'd carry you on his shoulder, and the pride would shine out of his eyes. Even then, you were the image of him – dark curly hair and big dark eyes, full of fun and laughter. Jack would never tire of playing with you and Davy. He was a hard worker, too, and he'd even take Davy to work with him, to keep him occupied.

'And I've just remembered your name! Sarah! How could I have forgotten! I'm very glad to have met you, Sarah, and to see that you've grown into a lovely young lady. Jack would have been so proud!'

I couldn't speak. There was so much I wanted to hear from Harry, but my throat was tight, and I could feel tears brimming in my eyes.

'Hey!' Harry said softly. 'Now I've gone and upset you. Like I said, it's reviving old memories. I shouldn't have done it.'

'Oh, Harry, please!' I begged. 'All my life, I've wanted someone to talk about my father, and no one ever will! People around here, when they know who I am, stop talking about him suddenly. *Why*, Harry?'

He frowned. 'I'm not right sure, love. Could be they're doubtful if you know about – well, what happened, or even, maybe, if you know what Jack really *was*. Everyone here remembers the terrible thing that happened, see? It's awkward if they think, maybe, you're too young to have been told about it.'

I bit my lip and took the biggest chance I'd ever taken in my life. 'Harry,' I said, 'I *don't* know what happened. All I know is that my father was killed in a shooting accident.'

He didn't speak for a moment, then he said, 'Yes. Well, that's what happened, Sarah.'

'But — how did it happen? Why can't I be told? What did you mean when you said, "What Jack really *was*"?'

'Well, Sarah, your family will have their reasons. It could be that your mother isn't able to speak about it, and I can understand that. Perhaps, if you were to ask your gran, quietly, when you were alone with her . . . You see, Sarah, it's not for an outsider like me . . .'

The silence seemed to stretch between us. The crackle of the fire sounded very loud. Fighting to control my disappointment, I said, 'It's all right, Harry. If you can't tell me, it doesn't matter. I've got a way of finding out the truth. On Monday I'm going to Charnley, to look at back copies of the local newspaper. There'll be a report of the accident, and of the inquest. So I'll know then.'

Harry stood up, crossed to the window and looked out. 'Fog's rolled right back now,' he said. 'I thought I heard a horse cantering. Yes! Why, it's the doctor's boy — young Greg Anderson. Looks as if he's coming here.'

'Oh! He must have come to meet me!' I cried, jumping up. 'I'll be back in a moment, Harry.'

I raced outside to see Greg turning into the yard on the piebald mare. He dismounted and hugged me. 'They'd saddled up to come looking for you,' he said. 'I asked if I could take this mare and come to meet you. I'd no idea you were caught in the fog, till I got to the farm. Are you all right? It must have been terrifying.'

As we tied the piebald mare up in the yard, I told him what Harry had said about my father, and how he wouldn't give any details about the shooting accident. I realized I still had the pink blanket draped around me. 'I'll get my jacket, and pay Harry for the phone call,' I said.

We went back into the inn to see Harry carrying a tray with three mugs on it. 'More coffee,' he said. 'And how are you, young Greg? Come and sit down.'

We followed him into the lounge, and he said, 'So you two are friends, are you?'

'I was just telling Greg,' I said, 'that you knew my father. He knows about people being unwilling to talk about him to me. He's taking me to Charnley to look at the newspapers.'

We sat down by the fire, Greg and I on the chester-field, Harry opposite us in a leather armchair. Harry looked at me intently' 'Sarah,' he said, 'I can't let that happen.'

I gazed back at him. 'What do you mean?'

'Not that way, love. Not his own daughter, that he loved so much, finding out about it in cold print, in some newspaper office, written the way the reporters saw it. I'll tell you, Sarah, for Jack's sake, and for yours.'

I wasn't sure I'd heard him correctly, but then Greg said softly, 'Maybe I ought not to be here.'

'Oh, *please* stay!' I grabbed his hand. Harry nodded.

It was very quiet in the low-ceilinged room, with the firelight twinkling on the brass ornaments. A log crackled, and I started, but Greg squeezed my hand gently.

Harry said, 'It happened the night Jack's family came for him. He'd always warned Sally, your mother, that it would happen, and told her she was to leave it to him to deal with them. But when they came, she defied them – ordered them out of the house. So they took you, Sarah, and that was the cause of it all.'

I blinked at him, completely baffled. 'I – I don't understand,' I frowned. 'Why did my father's family want him to leave the village?'

Harry stared into the fire for a long moment. 'So you don't even know that!' he sighed. 'And it's not my place to tell you – except, I can't have you reading them newspapers, not without knowing the truth.

'They was gypsies, love. Not didicoys, like we call ordinary travelling folk, but real Romanies, with their own laws, and customs, and language. Don't confuse them with ordinary gypsies, Sarah, because they wasn't. You could see it, to look at them. They was handsome people, proud and dignified.'

I couldn't take it in. It was crazy! My father, a gypsy? *My mother, married* to a *gypsy?* No! I mean, a joke was one thing, but this was ridiculous! Harry was still talking, just as if he'd happened to mention that one of my ancestors was Welsh and wore a bow-tie! I took a breath and tried to listen to his voice, deep and warm and comforting, like the pink blanket that enveloped me.

'I was told that when Jack first came to the village, everyone was surprised when he settled and stayed. The gypsies were camped in the woods, and Jim Richardson took Jack on as a cowman, expecting him to up and leave as suddenly as he'd appeared on the doorstep asking for work.

'But the gypsies left, and Jack stayed. The parents of the village girls were worried to death, with him being so handsome and all their daughters in love with him. They thought he'd whisk one of their girls off to a travelling life! They all gave a sigh of relief when he married Sally and their girls were safe.

'They needn't have worried. Jack had given up the travelling life. Mr Richardson thought a lot of him, and let him have Hawthorn Cottage to live in. It was falling down when Jack took it on, and he practically rebuilt it and made a pretty little house out of it.

'I couldn't let you read about Jack in the papers, love. Not without *knowing*. Them reporters made a lot of him being a gypsy — as if he were one o' them raggle-taggle ruffians you read about in stories: "Gypsy boy makes good" sort of romantic nonsense! Well, Jack didn't have to make good. He *was* good. I never knew anyone like him.'

He turned to me, his blue eyes worried. 'Have I done wrong, Sarah, telling you the truth?'

'I — I just can't take it in,' I murmured.

Greg said, 'How can it be wrong, Harry? We'd have found out on Monday anyway.'

I didn't hear Harry's reply. I was cut off. Everything seemed unreal. It was the same feeling I'd had after that awful dream in the woods. I found myself telling Harry and Greg about the dream, as if it was relevant, somehow. Maybe it was because it had been the sight of a bonfire that had brought me back to reality that day. Or because Harry had said that the gypsies were camped in the woods. Or just because the dream was as far out as the story I'd just heard.

Harry listened, nodding now and again. Then he said, 'The wide clearing as you go into the woods from Greenacres meadow? The place where there are beech trees at the top of a grassy slope that runs down to the beck?'

'Yes,' I answered. 'And across the stream, there's a weeping willow.'

'But, Sarah,' he said, 'that weren't exactly a dream. It was more like you was remembering, because what you dreamt is what happened on the night Jack died. Maybe you remembered because you were in the very spot where they camped that night, only it was a wide clearing then. The trees have grown into it now. Or maybe the woodsmoke brought the memory to life.

'Sally was alone in the cottage when they came, with you asleep upstairs. She forgot all what Jack told her, about leaving it to him to talk to them. She just said she wasn't going with them, and ordered them out of the house.

'Romanies take a lot of account of families, see? They hadn't expected Jack's wife to be hostile. They wanted Jack and Sally to have a "proper" Romany marriage before any discussion could take place, but Sally wasn't listening to them. While she was shouting at them to leave, one of them must have nipped upstairs and taken you.

'They left, and soon Jack came home and loaded his gun, ready to go rabbit-shooting. But then Sally came screaming down the stairs, having just discovered you was missing. Jack dropped the gun and ran off to the camp, telling Sally to wait at the cottage, promising to bring the baby back.

'Only Sally couldn't wait, see? What woman could, with her baby stolen? Especially knowing who'd taken it. She was hysterical, and she ran to the village carrying Jack's gun and screaming that the gypsies had taken her baby and someone must help her.

'About a dozen of us men got our shotguns and set off. Sally wouldn't stay in the village, with the other women. She came with us, crying all the time, begging us to get her baby back.

'When we got to the camp, the gypsy men came out and stood one side of their fire. We stood opposite, facing them. It was dark, but we could see them in the firelight. The local policeman had warned us there was to be no violence, but we took the guns to frighten them. He'd managed to take Jack's gun from Sally. She wouldn't have known how to fire it anyway. He leaned it against a tree, and he was holding Sally by the arm. She was still crying and trembling all over.

'Jack came across to our side of the fire and took hold of Sally, telling her there was nothing to worry about, pleading with her to stop us doing any violence, to give him a bit of time to talk to his people. He swore to her that he'd come home soon and bring the baby with him.

'But Sally couldn't listen to Jack, or to anyone. She only wanted her baby, and she pushed Jack away and struggled with him when he took hold of her again, still trying to talk to her calmly. Jack was a strong man, but he couldn't hold her, and she broke away from him to run to the caravans. Jack swung round to follow her, and tripped over the gun — or else he fell against it, where it was propped against the tree. The gun went off, and Jack fell dead.

'Even then, Sally didn't know what had happened. She went on running towards the caravans. She was beyond reason, see? She ran from one caravan to another until she found you, then she ran past us, carrying you. It was the policeman who shouted, "Let her go!" Someone must have tried to stop her. I didn't see, because I was kneeling down beside Jack — and there was nothing I or anyone else could do for him. Fancy you remembering those words, "Let her go!".'

He was silent for a moment, then he went on, 'Well, Sarah, that's what happened. It was a truly terrible thing. It still haunts me, the memory of that night. Your grandparents took you and Sally back to the farm. Sally was ill for weeks with the shock. Maybe now, you can understand why she can't talk about your father. Your grandad told me that she still doesn't like coming back here. She never stays long, does she? The memories are still too strong for her.'

A strange feeling of calm had come over me, replacing the sense of unreality. I said, 'So *that's* why my grandparents opposed the marriage! Because he was a gypsy!'

Greg's arm was around me. I could feel him so close beside me. I felt safe, protected.

'You can't blame your grandparents, Sarah,' Harry said. 'Well-brought-up girls don't run off to marry gypsies, except in songs! It wasn't until you knew Jack that you could sweep aside all your prejudice. Just knowing him made those notions seem ridiculous.'

'His parents,' I said wonderingly, 'would be my

other grandparents. Maybe they objected to the marriage, too. Did you see them? What did they look like?'

'They was dead, love,' Harry said. 'Maybe that was why Jack decided to settle. The rest of the family take responsibility for orphans, but maybe he felt he didn't belong no more.'

Quietly, Greg asked, 'What happened at the inquest?'

Harry said, 'The doctors wouldn't let Sally attend, Greg. We all testified to what happened. The verdict was accidental death. What else could it have been? When the policeman, Bob Jarvis, leaned that gun against the tree, he didn't know it was loaded. Sally wouldn't have known how to load it, and he thought she'd just grabbed it instinctively, and run out with it.'

'Harry,' I asked, 'what did the gypsies say, in court? How did they explain about taking a baby?'

'They don't trust our courts,' he replied. 'Jack's boss, Mr Richardson, got a solicitor to speak for them – to explain things, so that they only had to answer questions. He explained that in their eyes, according to their laws, they weren't guilty of abduction – not that anyone had put that charge – it was just explained so that we could understand.

'A Romany child belongs with a Romany family, so they said you had a right to be with them, to live their life, to learn their ways. Since a baby can't stand up for its rights, they took you – for *your* sake, see? Once they were satisfied that Jack and Sally had made up their minds to settle on the farm they'd have given you back and gone away. They just wanted to be sure – to make one last plea.

'It was very sad to see those men in court, Sarah. They behaved proud and dignified, but they was broken people. They answered questions carefully, quietly, and that was the last anyone saw of them.'

Now that I'd recovered from the shock, my mind was filled with questions. I had the feeling that there would never be another chance like this to find out all I needed to know.

'In the churchyard,' I said, 'there's no grave for my father. Was he cremated?'

Harry paused, looking at me uncertainly. 'Give me a minute to answer that, love,' he said. 'Cremation. Well, yes. The gypsies asked to be allowed to take him, and Sally agreed, because she understood why.

'Now, Sarah, I can't testify to the truth of this. It's what I've heard, and what the village believed happened. I've been told when a Romany dies, his body is burned and all his possessions with him. If he owns a caravan, he's placed in it and the caravan is burned to the ground. Nothing can be passed on — not even money, or jewellery. That's Romany law.'

I let the blanket slide from around my shoulders. The fire had warmed me, and I was aware of a sense of deep peace that I'd never known before. Now, at last, I knew the truth, and it was wonderful.

And then, for no reason at all, I was in tears, and Greg had pulled me close, to rest my head on his shoulder.

I heard Harry murmuring, 'I should have found some other way of telling you. But I'm only a plain sort of chap. If it came out rough and ready — it wasn't meant, Sarah.'

'No,' I sobbed. 'It was beautiful. Knowing things

were being kept from me – it was awful! I imagined terrible things. Now it's all over – and it's wonderful.'

Greg put his handkerchief into my hand and I dried my eyes.

Harry said, 'It's been good to talk about Jack. Seeing you, Sarah, with his dark eyes, and that open, friendly look – it brings him alive again.'

His voice changed slightly, and I blinked away my tears and gazed at him. 'And Sarah,' he said gruffly, 'don't you never, not for one moment, let anyone make you feel ashamed of what Jack was.

'He was the finest man I ever knew. Farmers from miles around would come to him for advice on their livestock. He had an instinct for animals, especially horses. Your grandad would never buy a horse without Jack had approved it first.'

'What?' I sat up straight, staring at him. 'I thought Gran and Grandad would have nothing to do with my father!'

Harry looked puzzled. 'Must have been at first, then, before I came here. Many an evening, a few of us would gather at Greenacres, and your gran would ask Jack to play his violin for us. Magic, it was! And I do know your grandad had planned to go over completely to breeding horses – to make Greenacres a stud farm, and take Jack as his partner. After Jack died, he seemed to lose heart. He said, without Jack, he didn't have the confidence to take the risks.'

'Then,' I gasped, 'why won't they talk about him? I've been afraid to speak of him.'

'Afraid?' Harry frowned. 'That's a tragedy!' He thought for a moment, then said, 'Not that I know, of course, but it could be Sally's doing. Well, she's made a very different life for herself – a life in which a Romany husband doesn't fit. Besides, as I said before, we all have prejudices, don't we – especially about things we don't understand, or know nothing about. When you were old enough to be told, she might have thought you were old enough to get a terrible shock when you heard the truth.'

'And you think Gran and Grandad would agree never to tell me that my father was a gypsy?'

'Could be,' he nodded. 'They'd maybe think you had to be more experienced in life before you could accept a thing like that.'

I sighed. 'I wish I knew what he looked like,' I said. 'You haven't got a photograph of him, have you, Harry?'

He smiled. 'I can do better than that. We had an artist come to stay at the inn, one summer. He'd come to paint the landscape, but when he saw Jack, he asked him to pose for a portrait. By the time he left, Jack was fair sick of sitting still to be painted. He did several really fine portraits of Jack, and he gave him what I think was the best one – because Jack wouldn't accept any payment for sitting. I'll go and fetch it for you.'

As Harry left the room, I closed my eyes. 'Greg,' I breathed, 'I'm going to know what he looked like – at last!'

He kissed me briefly. 'He looked like you. That means he was really something! No wonder the artist wanted to paint him!'

Harry came in, carrying a picture in a heavy, ornate frame, which he placed on the coffee table. I looked down at a head-and-shoulders portrait of a dark young man in a blue shirt, with a red scarf knotted carelessly at the throat. His dark eyes seemed to be alight with amusement, as if he was looking straight at me and sharing some secret with me. I found myself smiling in response, though my lips trembled with emotion.

'Could I come back with my camera, Harry? I'd like to take a photograph of this, to keep.'

'No need, love,' he smiled. 'It's yours.'

The stupid tears sprang to my eyes again. 'I couldn't take it,' I gasped. 'He gave it to *you*.'

Harry grinned. 'Jack gave it to me because he didn't want it. He took it out of politeness. He said he saw enough of his face in the mirror, shaving every morning. Sarah — I want you to have it.'

I blinked away my tears. 'But — he wouldn't want it handed down,' I said. 'Romany law — you told me—'

'Oh, Jack didn't bother with all that,' Harry chuckled. 'Sarah, I always wanted to do something for Jack, because of what he did for Davy. But there was nothing I could do that he'd accept. Now I can do something for his daughter. And Sarah — I don't need the picture, because I knew the man.'

'Thank you, Harry,' I whispered. 'I'd rather have this than anything on earth.'

'Well, you can't take it back on a horse,' he smiled. 'So I'll get one more visit out of you, when you come to collect it.'

'Harry, you'll be tired of me dropping in to see you,' I warned him. 'But we really ought to go now, I think.'

On the ride home, Greg turned to me with the smile that made my heart turn over. 'Now I can confess,' he said. 'I was dreading going to the newspaper office, thinking we'd discover something awful, and I'd be responsible!'

'I was terrified,' I admitted. 'But, Greg, I *had* to know, and I'll always be grateful to you for understanding and helping. Greg, I know how people — well, some people — feel about gypsies. Does it make you feel different about me?'

He laughed. 'Tell you one thing — it beats a chap at school who used to boast about being descended from Red Indians!'

I giggled. 'Now I know the answers,' I said, 'I've thought of a whole lot more questions. Like why on earth my mother ever thought she could settle for being a gypsy's wife — a farm labourer's wife in fact She hates country life, and she's so ambitious.'

'Maybe she was different then,' Greg said. 'Maybe it's what they call over-compensation.'

'What is?'

'Ambition. Some people are ambitious because they're trying to make up for something that's missing from their lives. I read that in a book on psychology.'

'Making up for losing my father?' I frowned. 'But she told me it was a terrible mistake; that my grandparents were right all the time.'

'She did? Could that have been a warning to you, not to get married too young? Trying to protect you?'

I shrugged. 'You're the one who's read the book,' I grinned.

We were near the farm now, and I said, 'Greg, I won't say anything to Gran and Grandad just yet. I haven't taken it in myself. I want to wait for the right moment.'

I was thinking, what if the events of that night had worked out differently? Not that I could imagine my mother as a country housewife. But how marvellous it would have been for me to grow up here, with my father!

'She should have told me about him,' I said suddenly. 'I had a right to know. He was her husband, but he was *my father* – my flesh and blood!'

Quietly, Greg said, 'She thought you were too young to handle it – remember?'

I knew what he meant was, 'Are you sure she wasn't right, if that's your reaction?'

'She was wrong,' I said. 'It was knowing nothing that I couldn't handle.'

I was beginning to understand things that had baffled me before. I'd tried hard to be what my mother wanted me to be, and felt guilty for failing. If I'd known about my father I'd have realized that I was like him in lots of ways: happier in the country than in the town, feeling close to animals and knowing that I understood them.

I'd thought it wouldn't be easy, getting through dinner without saying something about my new-found knowledge, but it was no problem. I felt strangely happy, and calm. We were sitting over coffee when the phone rang, and Gran said it would be Mum, for me.

I closed the dining-room door as I went into the hall and picked up the phone. I answered Mum's questions, asked about the conference, then I took a deep breath and said, 'Mum, if Gran agreed for me to stay here longer – more than this fortnight, I mean – would you mind?'

There was a pause. 'Sarah, haven't you forgotten something? Like Florida?'

'Well, that's it, you see. Actually, I'd rather stay here.'

My heart was hammering in my chest as I gripped the receiver.

'*What*? Stay on the farm, rather than go to the States?'

'I'm sorry, Mum, if it sounds ungrateful. I'm sure it does.'

There was a long pause, and I said, 'Mum – are you still there?'

She answered, 'Oh! I've just worked it out! You've met a boy there, haven't you? The one you used to play with . . . Tom. Is that the reason?'

'It's Greg, not Tom,' I replied. 'He's not the whole reason, though. It just seems silly to spend all that money on me when I don't really want to go. It's not that I'm not grateful—'

'No need to be grateful. Don't you realize that you'll miss the opportunity of seeing new places, meeting interesting people? There's always someone of your own age, isn't there? I know it can't be much fun with me and Aunt Jane . . .'

So she was going to agree! 'Mum – can you get the money back, for the air fare and everything?'

She laughed lightly. 'I expect so. You'd better ask Gran if you can stay there. If she agrees, phone Aunt Jane and get her to cancel for you. But think it over carefully first. No use changing your mind later, when everything's reorganized.'

She was always hinting that I made rash decisions which I regretted later. It wasn't true.

When I returned to the dinner table, Grandad smiled

and said, 'If you were a little girl again, I'd think you were up to something. That sparkle in your eyes — you've had it all through dinner.'

We all laughed as my cheeks turned bright pink, then I said, 'Mum says I needn't go to Florida, provided I can stay here instead.'

Gran exclaimed, 'Well, of course you can! But — are you quite sure you want to? I mean, we can't compete with Florida.'

'Yes we can,' Grandad grinned. 'Greg and I can get some Bermuda shorts, and some of those brightly coloured shirts, and wear them around the place.'

'You'll frighten the horses!' Gran said. 'I hope Sally isn't upset about it.'

I felt Greg's hand take mine, under the table. As my fingers closed around his, I said, 'I'm sure she isn't. She won't have to worry all the time about whether I'm enjoying myself or not.'

It was the first time I could remember ever doing something I wanted to do, rather than what had been decided for me. Why had it taken so much courage?

'You've certainly had an eventful day,' Grandad smiled.

'More than you realize,' I said, looking at him across the table. I plunged ahead while I still had some courage left. 'After getting lost in the fog on the moors, I met Harry, and he told me that my father was a gypsy.'

The smiles died on my grandparents' faces. There was utter silence in the room and, under the table, Greg squeezed my hand gently.

Grandad sighed heavily. 'I always knew it would happen like this. I warned Sally so often, so did Jane.

Well, Sarah, how do you feel about it?'

'Relieved,' I said, and then I told them of the awful things I'd imagined because no one would tell me the truth. I saw Grandad's face grow dark with anger, and Gran looked away, as if she couldn't bear to think about it.

I went on to explain that I'd arranged to look at back copies of newspapers to find out about my father's death, and that Harry had told me the truth to save me from reading the newspaper reports.

Grandad murmured, 'All this because your mother couldn't risk your telling her sophisticated friends that she'd been married to a gypsy! My God! These days, I'd have thought it would be a plus! Shock value. Something to toss off in the middle of a cocktail party for everyone to say, "How exciting, darling!" '

'Don't be so hard on Sally, John,' Gran said. 'I'm sure that's not the reason. She cut Jack's memory out of her life, because that was the only way she could go on. You remember how she was, John, for all those weeks – couldn't eat or sleep. The doctors—'

'I remember!' Grandad snapped, as if it was something he didn't want to think about. 'But she did recover, in time. I never did agree that Sarah shouldn't be told about Jack.'

'She did tell me some things,' I said. 'Like that you opposed the marriage.'

'They were too young,' Gran said. 'At sixteen, Sally was still a child, not like Jane, who was quite mature at that age. Jack was twenty, in some ways adult and responsible, in others still a boy.'

Grandad said, 'We thought Jack would want to be off, travelling some day, and that sort of life would have been no good to Sally. Of course, we just didn't know Jack – not then.'

'Harry told me so much about him,' I said. 'He sounds really too good to be true. I suppose that's because Harry liked him a lot.'

Grandad shook his head. 'No, Sarah. Jack *was* too good to be true. You might meet someone like him once in your life, if you're lucky. When I first met him he was a scruffy young lad, taking too much interest in my daughter. Later, when I knew him, I discovered that he was the sort of man I'd have liked for a son.'

I'd told them about the portrait Harry had given me. 'I've always thought it strange,' I said, 'that there were no photos.'

'Sally didn't want you to see any photos of Jack,' Gran said. 'She didn't want you to be curious about him. But I took lots of photos. They're in a box up in the loft with your old baby furniture. I'll go and get them.'

Why hadn't I ever looked in those boxes in the loft? I scolded myself. I'd never dreamed they held such treasures.

Gran came back with an album of photographs. There were family groups with all of us in them, and lots of pictures of me with my father, and with a little Shetland pony he'd bought for me. Mum looked so different – long hair and ordinary clothes – and she looked so happy, as if she was always laughing.

Grandad went out of the room while we were looking at the photographs, and came back with two very old and battered instrument cases. One contained my father's violin; the other his flute. 'The violin is very old,' he said. 'I believe Jack's great-grandfather bought it in Italy. The Romanies travelled all over Europe, you know. His grandfather gave him both these instruments. They're yours now, Sarah.'

I took the violin out of its case, and held it gently. 'You'll need new strings,' Gran said. 'And I'm sure Sally will arrange for you to have lessons at school.'

'Is it really mine?' I whispered, fondling the burnished wood, thinking, *This was part of him. He could make wonderful music with this.* 'Is it mine, to keep?'

'It's yours,' Grandad nodded. 'They're both yours. Maybe one day you'll be able to bring them to life, as he could.'

It was beginning to grow dark when Greg and I took the dogs out for their evening run. We threw sticks for them in the meadow, and I said, 'Greg, I'm sorry – you must have been bored out of your mind with all this family talk!'

'*Bored*?' he echoed. 'It was fascinating! At home, there's just Dad and me, and Mrs Hunter who comes in daily. No dead heroes. No dark secrets kept for years. And, Sarah, how could I ever be bored, when you're here with me?'

He took me in his arms and kissed me. I felt as if I was floating on a cloud of happiness. If only he'd say he loved me, then there was nothing more in the world that I could possibly wish for! Surely, soon . . .?'

'I suppose I must be deadly boring,' he murmured, 'to you, with your wild gypsy blood.'

I fell against him, laughing. We laughed so much we had to support each other. When I recovered, I said, 'If I'm half gypsy, why can't I tell fortunes? I'd know then if you were coming to St Barnabas' in September. Is it too much to hope for, Greg?'

'Probably, but that needn't stop us hoping,' he grinned. 'Meantime, think of all the time we've got together now! Weeks and weeks!'

The dogs were back with the sticks, demanding attention. We threw them, and Greg put his arm around my shoulders and drew me close. My arm was around his waist, my head against his shoulder. The dogs were bounding away through the long grass and the sun was beginning to set, touching the treetops with gold.

'Oh, Sarah! I love you so much,' Greg sighed.

I closed my eyes, filled with almost unbearable joy. 'I love you, too, Greg.' I replied softly.

# Afterwards

There's more. Six weeks ago, I'd have said that was the end of the story, then something else happened, something important – to me, anyway.

But first, Greg didn't get into St Barnabas'. He was accepted for St John's, which was his second choice, and St John's is in Paddington, only a short tube ride from where I live. It's a smaller hospital, but Aunt Jane says it's just as good as Barney's, and Greg's quite happy about it.

I'd been dreading the day when Mum would come to take me home and I'd have to tell her I'd found out about my father. Whatever Gran said, I couldn't forgive her.

She arrived on a Friday evening, looking marvellous with a deep golden tan, in a white linen suit and royal-blue silk blouse. I'm no good at acting. I couldn't pretend I was overjoyed to see her, and Gran and Grandad seemed preoccupied, weighed down with the thought of the confrontation ahead.

We'd waited dinner for Mum, and there were these long silences during the meal. Mum would have had to be stupid not to know something was wrong – and she isn't stupid! After one of the silences, Grandad said, 'Hawthorn Cottage is for sale.'

I knew this. Alison had told me. The Bartons, who lived there, had an aunt in the village who'd died and left them her house, so they'd moved out and the farmer who owned the cottage wanted to sell it.

Mum said it would be nice for the Bartons to have the security of their own home. Not a word to me about how we used to live there. Anger boiled up inside me.

We took our coffee into the living room, and Mum said, 'Right. I know I'm going to be told something I won't like. Who'll start?'

Gran and Grandad looked at each other. I looked at the carpet. *Let her go on wondering for a bit,* I thought. *See how* she *likes it.* Then Gran told her everything, and Grandad said, 'Lucky it was Harry who told her. Could have been anybody. I always warned you, Sally—'

'Not a lecture tonight, Dad, please,' said Mum, looking pale and tense. 'It's late, and I'm tired. Let's discuss this in the morning.'

I said, 'You can discuss it whenever you like, but not with me.' Then I said good night and went to bed.

Mum didn't get up to breakfast next morning, but when I was in the stables, at about ten o'clock, I saw her drive off somewhere. Later, when I went into the kitchen for coffee, she was there. She said, 'Sarah, after coffee, I want you to come with me to see Hawthorn Cottage.'

'I've seen it,' I said.

'Sarah – *please*,' Mum murmured. 'This is important.'

We didn't speak all the way to the cottage, until Mum turned the car on to the rough track, and I muttered, 'Won't this ruin the springs?'

'Springs?' she shrugged. 'What are springs *for*?'

The sun was blazing down, and the little house looked so pretty, but a bit forlorn without curtains, and the grass under the May tree needed cutting.

Mum said, 'I got the keys from Mr Lockwood. I thought you'd like to see inside.'

'Why would I want to do that?' I muttered, although I was really dying to.

Mum sighed. 'You were born here, one winter's night. Your little Shetland pony lived in the field behind the house. That's the May tree your father planted on the day you were born.'

'But my father was a gypsy, and you were ashamed of him. You forgot all about him when he died. So let's skip the nostalgia trip.'

She looked as if I'd stabbed her. She got out of the car, walked through the white gate, and went to lean against the May tree. It was hot in the car, so I got out too. She said, 'Sarah, we have to talk about this.'

'Really?' I scoffed. 'After all these years, it's suddenly urgent?'

'You've got it wrong,' she said. 'I was never ashamed of him. And I never forgot him, not for one day. Even if I'd wanted to, how could I, when you look at me with his eyes, and turn your head the way he used to . . .'

She slid down to sit on the grass under the May tree. Her hair was tousled. She looked tired, and sort of — vulnerable.

I sat down in the shade beside her. 'OK,' I said. 'Let's talk. First, let me tell you what I imagined when you refused to talk about my father.' I described the terrors I'd endured, and she stared at me, then hid her face in her hands and murmured, 'Oh, my *God*!'

She took her hands away, and there were tears in her eyes! I couldn't believe it! Mum never cries.

'I loved him so much,' she whispered. 'We were part of each other. When he died, part of me died, too. I knew I had to survive, to make a good life for you. I could only do it by getting away from here, to a place where there were streets and buildings instead of trees and fields — where I couldn't see sympathy on the face of everyone I met. I was an actress, playing a part. I became a damned good actress, but I never stopped being afraid.'

I stared at her. '*You? Afraid?* Of *what*?'

'Of what I did,' she said, 'when I was young and silly and at the mercy of my emotions. I suppose Harry told you how Jack died?'

I nodded.

'They took my baby,' she said. 'I had to get you back. That's all I knew. I don't remember picking up the gun, though I know, at some time, that I was carrying it. I remember Jack's face in the light from the camp fire. He was talking to me. I saw his lips moving, but I couldn't hear him. I just had to find you. I remember searching the caravans for you, finding you, running home with you . . .'

She closed her eyes and went on: 'I didn't know Jack was dead. I didn't even know *that*! When I got back to the cottage with you, your grandad's car was outside. He took us home to Greenacres. They came and told us Jack was dead . . . I've no memory of the next few weeks. I think I died, too, for a while. I wanted to die, and then I knew that I had to try to make it up to you, somehow.'

She opened her eyes and looked at me. 'I wanted to

tell you about him, Sarah. I wanted to, *so much*! But I couldn't. Don't you see? I took him from you. If I hadn't taken the gun . . .'

'No, Mum!' I gasped. 'You didn't know what you were doing! It wasn't your fault!'

Tears were streaming down her face. 'I've tried, all my life,' she said, 'to make it up to you, to give you a good life. I could never talk about him, because of the guilt. I had to pretend there was nothing missing in our lives. I made a different life for us. It's a good life. It's fine – so long as I don't let myself remember.'

I put my arms around her and we clung together, crying.

'I'm sorry,' I choked. 'I thought— Oh, Mum, you *have* made a good life for me. You *have*!'

'*No*! I got it all *wrong*! You're so like him . . . But I couldn't stay here, where everything reminded me of him. Instead, I had to try to make you fit into another kind of life. As you grew up, you became even more like him, so I tried harder.'

She found a hanky, and offered it to me. 'You first,' I sniffed.

She mopped her eyes. 'I couldn't come back to this house after Jack died, for a long time. When I did gather enough courage to come, I couldn't go inside. Today, I thought, I must do it, with you. And I thought I could, because with you, I've never shown fear or weakness. And yet, it seems . . .'

'You want to go inside?' I whispered.

She pushed her hair back. 'I dream about it. I think of the little kitchen, where we'd sit together in the long dark evenings, just talking, for hours; the view from the back bedroom window . . .'

'Come on then,' I said shakily, standing up. Slowly, she got to her feet. 'The keys,' I murmured.

She gave them to me. I took her hand, and we walked to the front door. I fitted the key into the lock, still holding Mum's hand. We stepped inside, into a tiny lobby, with stairs leading up and a door on our left.

Mum shivered. 'It's so cold,' she murmured.

It was cool, after the hot sun outside, but it wasn't cold.

'It's been empty three weeks,' I said. 'Probably damp. Is the kitchen through here?' I led the way to the back of the house.

In the kitchen there was a small circular table made of dark oak, with four matching chairs, the backs intricately carved to match the pattern around the edge of the table. 'You'd think the Bartons would want to take these, wouldn't you?' I said.

Mum was running her fingers along the smooth top of the table. 'They were renting,' she said. 'They'd have to leave whatever was here when they came. I'm glad these are still here. I want them. He made these.'

We stayed in the cottage for ages. Mum showed me the stone fireplace my father had built, and the carved staircase he'd made, and told me lots of things about him – like how he used to ride Grandad's horses bareback.

'Are you going to have the table and chairs sent back home?' I asked, wondering where they'd fit into the flat.

She didn't answer for a moment, then she said, 'I'd like to buy the cottage. We could use it for weekends and odd holidays. When you're older, you could come, bring your friends . . .'

'But,' I frowned, 'you don't like coming here. I mean – I'd love it, but—'

We were in the back bedroom, with the casement window open, looking out across the fields. 'I think,' she said, 'it's going to be all right now. That is, if you can forgive me.'

'Oh, Mum!' We were in each other's arms again. 'I just didn't understand,' I said.

'How could you?' she sighed. 'And why should you have to? Sarah, I'm so grateful to you. I thought I could live by shutting myself away from the truth, letting myself feel nothing. But you opened that front door for me . . . It was like coming home. All the memories are here. I need them now. They belong to you, too. I want to share them with you.'

I suppose that isn't really the end, either, because it's a sort of new beginning. Another story. A happier one.

# Mary Hooper
## Blondes Have More Fun And Other Stories £1.25

In *Blondes Have More Fun*, Melly is afraid that Kinde, the gorgeous blonde German exchange student who's coming to stay at her house, will spoil her chances with Ian, the boy next door. But there's a surprise in store – especially for Ian . . .

There's a surprise of a different sort in *Days of Darkness* when Cassie, who's just beginning to get over the death of her boyfriend Rob, suddenly receives a belated birthday card – from Rob.

And in *I Can Still See His Eyes*, Tina falls in love with Mike, despite his reputation for being a bit of a lad. But the day she decides to have a heart-to-heart talk with him is also the day she discovers he's seeing someone else . . .

There are nine more great stories of young love in this super collection by one of *Heartlines'* favourite authors. Some of them have a light humorous touch, others are longer stories with a darker side. They are all wonderfully entertaining.

# Jane Pitt
## The Boy Who Was Magic £1.25

*"Who Janus is or what Janus is I haven't a clue! He's just somebody I met who plays a pink plastic whistle . . . He can play anything from Mozart to Mick Jagger on it, and when he whistles the world lights up. I fell in love with him and he gave me lavender. And now I've fallen in love with Rob"*

Jilly met Janus in the Spring and was instantly enchanted. Immediately she decided that the one thing she didn't want to do was to become a secretary, and much to her parents' dismay she left college. Rob, her old friend, thought she ought to start writing again, and Janus agreed.

They went around as a threesome that Summer: Jilly hadn't realized before that it was possible to be in love with two men at once, or that there were different kinds of love.

But her best friend Meg was jealous, and in a dangerous mood. At Meg's party, everything changed. Janus – like his namesake, the guardian of gates and doorways – pointed both Meg and Jilly towards new openings . . .

All these books are available at your local bookshop or newsagent, or can be ordered direct from the publisher. Indicate the number of copies required and fill in the form below.

Send to: **CS Department, Pan Books Ltd., P.O. Box 40, Basingstoke, Hants. RG21 2YT.**

or phone: 0256 469551 (Ansaphone), quoting title, author and Credit Card number.

Please enclose a remittance* to the value of the cover price plus: 60p for the first book plus 30p per copy for each additional book ordered to a maximum charge of £2.40 to cover postage and packing.

*Payment may be made in sterling by UK personal cheque, postal order, sterling draft or international money order, made payable to Pan Books Ltd.

Alternatively by Barclaycard/Access:

Card No. 

Signature:

Applicable only in the UK and Republic of Ireland.

*While every effort is made to keep prices low, it is sometimes necessary to increase prices at short notice. Pan Books reserve the right to show on covers and charge new retail prices which may differ from those advertised in the text or elsewhere.*

NAME AND ADDRESS IN BLOCK LETTERS PLEASE:

............................................................................................................................

Name ————————————————————————————

Address ————————————————————————————

————————————————————————————

————————————————————————————

————————————————————————————

3/87